PIRANESI'S DREAM

PIRANESI'S
DREAM

a novel by

GERHARD KÖPF

translated from the German by Leslie Willson

GEORGE BRAZILLER   NEW YORK

Originally published in Germany in 1992 by Luchterhand Literaturverlag GmbH
under the title *Piranesis Traum*

First published in the United States of America in 2000 by George Braziller, Inc.

For information, please address the publisher:
George Braziller, Inc.
171 Madison Avenue
New York, NY 10016

Library of Congress Cataloging-in-Publication Data:
Köpf, Gerhard, 1948–
    [Piranesis Traum. English]
    Piranesi's dream / by Gerhard Köpf ; translated from the German by Leslie Willson.
    p. cm.
    Includes bibliographical references.
    ISBN 0-8076-1473-4
    1. Piranesi, Giovanni Battista, 1720–1778—Fiction. I. Willson, A. Leslie (Amos Leslie), 1923–
        II. Title.
PT2671.O548 P5713 2000
833'.914—dc21   99-087741

Designed by Christopher Moisan

Printed and bound in the United States of America

First edition

All the so-called Old Masters are,
of course, failures. Without exception
all of them were condemned to fail,
and in every detail of their work the
observer can establish that failure . . .
—Thomas Bernhard

And when they find me one day with my mouth full of dry, red sand, then in front of the grave that I dug with my last strength they will see the tombstone that I cut from a stone I found, modeled after the heads of Easter Island. Perhaps it will just begin to grow dark, and the shadows will brush over the distant mountains like waves until they become one with the fleeing clouds in the darkening night. They will be amazed at the wasted desolation of the place, and there will be disquiet in their eyes at the sight of the fallen walls, of this avalanche of martyred ashlars. The reflection of the sun's finale will succeed in laying a unique enchantment over the scene, a curiously beaming stage light. No bird will fly up and away, no smoke rise into the sky, nothing but quiet and solitude will be there. Only the wind will play its forlorn game with the thin clumps of grass and the brush on the edge of the desert. They will not be able to imagine that someone could have lived here surrounded by so much abandonment and forgetting. Who, except for me, could endure so much solitude and bitterness so completely alone for so many years? For a long while in the midst of the stillness they will look at this dilapidated house, these weathered ruins, this rank, completely ramshackle cottage. The dilapidation and the dusk will confound their eyes, but no one will think of breaking the unchanging quiet and call out my name. But this stubborn quiet will give them the certainty that they have finally found me. The groaning of a rusty bar, which will yield under the pressure of their hands, and the beam of a flashlight will deliver the last proofs to them. A penetrating pestilential odor of rottenness and decay will surround them, and from that moment on, everything will take place with indifferent inevitability. A beat of black wings will be around them when they find me at the back with my clothes on, lying in a corner on a bed, my face turned condescendingly toward them, with my eye sockets empty, the eyes devoured by birds. Someone will light a candle and set it on the little table next to the cot. With stony faces they will stand around me, their hands protectively over their genitals. As soon as night has finally fallen, sitting at the kitchen table among all my papers, copperplates, etching needles, drawings, and plans they will reminisce about me, and tell the story about the man who himself wants to build a house: *Exemplum de quodam homine, qui volebat aedificare domum . . .*

Yes, that's how they'll find me and they'll say:

A man wants to build a house. He looks for a promising construction site, drafts a plan, and calculates the required capital of time and labor. But hardly has he begun with the excavation than it turns out that the ground thought to be solid is in truth marshy. This sad discovery presents the man with having to decide either to continue the construction in spite of the questionable soil and to leave its stability to a higher providence—or to spend a large part of his capital in shoring up the foundation, faced with the certainty that his building won't even get as far as the second floor.

A house of cards or a skeletal structure?

I always knew: I had to build!

There must be something or other in my brain that cannot quit thinking up structures that no one wants to build. But it's not the activity itself that so possesses me, rather it is the dream of it. In a corner of my heart sits something that has a similarity to religion.

It is in thrall to an adoration that my imagination always supplies with new nourishment.

In this world one can experience only two kinds of great happiness: that of loving very much or that of building. But most unhappy is he who is crushed with desire between these two realms.

I knew that I had to build!

But they didn't let me.

I never did build, on the contrary was always merely lost in thought.

I am an *inètto,* one unfit in an unfit world.

It is unendurable not to make the most of one's dreams.

I doubted everything, I despaired about everything, but not about the art of building. A good master builder always thinks beyond his buildings. Outside of building there is no salvation and no redemption. The art of building is the physical expression of my being. In this mine I am at home; I bring ever new treasures to the surface. And the highest commandment is my own dissatisfaction. Whatever we do, we remain the victims of our passion. We are in a dream, lying halfway above and halfway below the earth, and our dreaming minds are impenetrable. With comical despair I, a spendthrift of my pains, have never surrendered my belief that I was chosen by destiny for something that lay beyond the timberline of other master builders. Such a belief cannot be acquired but grows like a tree whose crown strives skyward while the roots grow down into the past.

With my unconditional belief in architecture I was an audacious man even to my contemporaries. All my life the rumor went around that because my failures turned into fury I had tried to murder my teacher, Guiseppe Vasi, because he had supposedly withheld from me the mysteries of the art of etching.

What wild nonsense, since no one knows those mysteries better than I.

The things they said about me:

Un homme d'un autre siècle, a *génie visionaire.*

There was talk of extraordinary talent, of unintelligibility and a demonic spirit. Just recently a so-called expert went so far as make the following judgment: *He was a strange and neurotic genius and difficult to handle, but he was a brilliant draughtsman and one of the greatest masters of the art of etching.*

Wrong, all wrong, for most statements about art come from people who are themselves not artists: thus the distorted notions! In any case, I have never been honored in a way that corresponds to my merits. To this very day I am branded with the mark of Cain as an artistic person running amok who stood outside his age, misunderstood, eccentric, and pathological:

He reveled in what was ugly and distorted.

He had a passionate, even a demonic nature.

The mystery of the sublime is his field.

That sort of nonsense is particularly the result of my depictions of prisons and especially the echo of Romantic poets. On closer examination such ridiculous judgments, however, prove to be evidence of sweeping perplexity.

I am the consequence of my history. But this history by no means satisfies me. A history is made only to be forgotten. I know, and I feel, that I have deserved better and do not want to forgo my claim. I base my value worth precisely on the fact that my ego, as a product of history, does not satisfy me. But that means that my history becomes the history of my distortion and I turn against it—so I gain freedom in the face of my history.

The most important men of my age knew about me. They all were delighted with my plans, and my teacher released me with the words: "If you stay longer with me, you will become my imitator. So move on, find your own way, and you will immortalize your name without any effort on my part."

I obeyed, but my misfortune began with my respect for authority. Money became scarce. I could find work nowhere. More and more often I withdrew to my drunkard's bed, believing the solution to my problems lay hidden in a bottle. I crouched in the blanket of my melancholy and felt life sliding away from me.

In vain I presented my sketches to the Roman emperor, to the king of France, to the popes, cardinals, princes, and potentates. All gave me audience, all were enthusiastic, all approved of what I was doing. They esteemed me as a man who had the power and the ability to affix obscure names to famous monuments.

But when it came to the construction itself, they postponed it from year to year: "Yes, when the financial situation improves . . ."

Thinking that I would not live long enough to complete a construction, even if someone should entrust me with a project of some magnitude, I decided very early on to have my designs printed, something disgraceful to my contemporaries. All of my etchings, the underwater paintings of someone submerged all his life, are no more than a reproach. I cast them down in front of my contemporaries as one casts down a piece of meat before a predator. Of course, I knew it was a folly that would be used against me sooner or later, for it is a crime to reveal your own dreams and visions. But I did not hesitate to commit that crime.

Zealously I set to work, sat day and night over my etchings. My designs went forth into the world and aroused laughter here, astonishment there. All the things that were said about me! Exaggerated sense of mission, hubris, megalomania, eccentric way of life, abrupt outbursts of passion, finally even a pact with the Devil.

Everything sheer calumny!

Everything pure nonsense!

People never understood how to read my works, for my scenes and etchings, designs and plans should not only be looked at but be read conscientiously.

But who can still read conscientiously today?

And something else was happening to me. Through bitter experience I had learned that with every work that springs from the mind of an artist a tormenting spirit is born, and every picture, every line that is drawn by chance on paper serves such a spirit as an abode. Those are evil spirits. They enjoy life, multiply incessantly, and torment their creator because of the too-cramped dwelling he offers them.

Hardly had I started to close my eyes than specters in the shapes of stately homes, palaces, buildings, castles, ruins, vaults, and columns surrounded me. All together they pressed upon me with their mighty masses and with horrible laughter asked me to give them life.

Life!

From that moment on I have known no peace. The specters created by me persecute me. There an enormous vault embraces me, here towers chase along behind me with mile-long strides, and now a window rattles before me in its gigantic frame. At times they lock me in my own dungeons, lower me down into bottomless wells, shackle me in my own chains, let the cold mildew of half-destroyed vaults rain down upon me—they make me endure all the torments I have invented. They toss me from the funeral pyre onto the rack and from the rack onto the spit. And all the while these horrors dance laughing around me, will not let me die, and try ever anew to find out why I have condemned them to an incomplete life. And finally, weak and enfeebled as I am, they push me back again and whip me at my own drawing table.

My outrageous power of imagination, all the wriggling thoughts everywhere in my mind have encircled me and surrounded me with bitterness and hardship. They have placed me in darkness and walled me in. In this darkness I make my rounds along the walls of my imagination and feel how something is happening beyond the inclines. Befogged by my task, I sneak into the walls, fit myself to them spinelessly with a naked, surrendered face. On the nape of my neck I feel that I'm being observed. It stiffens and I duck as though I were expecting the lethal bite of a predatory cat that takes measure of what was promised it and eagerly devours what it desires.

I, however, live recklessly. I live contrarily. My days are eaten up by the burning hunger of that cat. With every year my gaze is directed more exclusively into the distance. Only in this darkness am I moored totally within myself and feel even peaceful and safe for deceptive moments. So I am completely at home when the blackness warms me, as only animals can be completely at home with themselves. Then on the edge of my exhausted years the wilderness in my imagination becomes rampant through the tricks of my enemies, while outside of me roaring centuries pass by in which I hear nothing but the gnawing of my tormenting spirits, the clinking of their chains, their scraping and scratching on walls and ashlars that I was not allowed to build.

I was present already when that Great Wall was built that can be seen even from the moon. In the year 33 the Xiongnu were beaten back in the northwest. From Yu Yong on, along the Huang Ho and on to the east and connecting with Yin Shan they built border fortifications. The emperor further commanded Meng Tian to cross the Huang Ho and take possession of Kao'kue, of the

To Mountains, and of the middle part of the northern valley. There he built fortifications and watchtowers in defense against the Qiang. Convicts then populated the regions. In the year 34 the emperor cast out to work on the Long Wall judges who had handed down unjust sentences. The Great Wall was the ruin of one generation and the salvation of many, the Chinese say. But it was above all a mistake, for not the enemies from the north but the emperor's son destroyed the empire.

So I wander in vain from land to land, and each one becomes my galley. In vain I keep watch to see whether perhaps some splendid building erected by my rivals to ridicule me has collapsed. I knock on Michelangelo's dome in Rome in vain, in vain I hang with both arms in Pisa on Buschetto's useless tower. Sometimes I dream of moving, secretly at night, the Tower of Pisa to Venice and the Campanile of Venice to Pisa, the Eiffel Tower to London and the Tower of London to Paris, yes, all the towers of the world back and forth in accordance with the royal game, for chess is the only game that you can also play against yourself without destroying its meaning.

Towers, nothing but towers.

They fascinated me even in my childhood, and what child doesn't put block on block to build a tower, though it will never be clear whether a child is enthused more by the building or by the destruction of those towers. Towers have always attracted me magically, and on all my journeys I have never missed climbing the most famous towers. And even as a child I liked best to listen to the stories of collapsing towers that were felled by lightning, conflagration, or earthquake. At the same time always thinking—there are no boundaries upward.

So I knew I had to build.

Instead of executing a construction contract, I sat for days, weeks, months, years over my etchings. I constantly tried in vain to find out the causes for my frustrated life, and still got no further. I brooded about what I might have done differently, better, or possibly not at all. But it led to nothing. Catastrophe is inevitable, I told myself, and I had peace for a short time. Then I started all over again to ask myself all kinds of penetrating questions.

Restlessly I strode back and forth and up and down in my more and more wretched quarters. With my temples pressed against floors and walls I watched the turning of millions of light years, and rare orb-shaped heavenly bodies danced before my eyes. I had driven my life so far into isolation that there was no return from it. More and more I lapsed into senseless activities to distract me from my plans. Sometimes I locked my etchings and copperplates away in order not to come into contact with them, for new ideas came to me only when it was gloomy. But the very thought of them depressed me even further. The lack of contact developed into a catastrophe, just as it had previously been necessity and even happiness. The recognition of being able to build absolutely nothing, nothing, made my predicament even more hopeless.

I always knew—I *had* to build!

But a satanic God, who, with furiously clenched teeth, sits sullenly over His Creation, cast on my dream path just short of my destination a giant red stumbling block called Ayers Rock, with which especially the setting sun wreaks terrible things. Presumably He hurled it against me with all the furious malice of which a god is at all capable—because He could not help fearing that He had met His master in me. At the same time I had finally found the ideal construction site in the Australian desert and with

it that place where I could have made my visions reality. All my
life I have looked for this endless flat wilderness and believed that
Nature was finally on my side. For Nature has no respect for life.
But in the worst possible way I nevertheless had to recognize how
the elements, which I had set out to challenge and to harness, had
become allied against me behind my back.

And it had to come this far, and maybe it had long been preor-
dained, since that long-ago day when human beings first felt the
desire to want to live a life different from their own wretched life
in order to make up for all their missed opportunities. And from
that point on, I was lost, for in that moment the wind of disaster
began to blow. From that point on there remained for me only the
possibility of telling my story.

Oh, I know people. I know everything that crawls and grazes under the lash of God's whip. People resemble those who are drowning and who strike out wildly all around and simply hasten their sinking. I still trusted people when I had long known that they laugh at me, despise me, and in the nastiest way deceive me—yes, that they have only waited for the opportunity to destroy me.

I am not a popular artist. That doesn't sadden me, for I have never had the ambition to work for the all-powerful riffraff on the street.

You don't have to saw open human heads to realize that only disaster nests and catastrophes brood in them. I have always been deceived by everyone. I was incessantly deceived by my wife, by my friends, by just everyone. Life is nothing but a great plot to put one over on me. It's a comedy of flimflam. I believe only in misfortune and that being alive is debt enough for us to accept the bill and pay the price.

The bill: *Il conto.* Or *la dolorosa,* as the Romans say.

I don't belong to the whore-faced masses, I belong to myself. So I have no other choice than to look around inside myself after death. My deathly pale insides cry out for an animal death for my animal body and rebel against this suspended animation that has languished for several hundred years already.

Death pounds on my temples.

I say: Come in.

But he doesn't enter.

I'm still breathing.

It is well known that two things loosen the tongue: love, when it comes suddenly—and death, when it vacillates. That's why old men talk only to themselves. The art of soliloquy is a much higher art than the art of dialogue, someone once said, I've forgotten who it was. Every person whose madness has remained unobserved so far and whose state of distraction never surfaced winds up talking to himself. A thinking person will necessarily arrive at a soliloquy, for the thinker always finds himself in a gigantic orphanage in which it is constantly proven to him that he is without parents. Mind you, I'm speaking of an orphanage, not of a structure of thought.

I always wanted to build a structure of thought, and I didn't even manage to get as far as an orphanage. There wasn't enough, either for an architect of an orphanage or for an architect of a structure of thought. And I tried all my life to call to the heart of people with my work. But they didn't hear me.

Not a single person has ever conveyed something that might have been the truth. But I have never given up the attempt to convey the truth. Still, honesty proves to me that there is no truth, nor can there be.

Come with me! On our way I will tell you my fearful story, but I can't look you in the eye too long, for the longer we look into the eyes of a human being, the more maimed he seems to us.

But what am I saying! It's all a waste of breath. A lot of words point to the land of Futility.

Futility has become the main word of my life.

Time passed by, buildings begun were finished, my rivals gained immortality. But I wandered from court to court, from anteroom to anteroom, hung around humbly before I was humbled

in those anterooms of forgetfulness, stood there with my portfo-
lio that was more and more filled for naught with beautiful and
impracticable designs. How many courtyards without sunlight
have I since entered, restlessly wandering about in my inexhaustible museum of shades!

Must I tell you what I felt when with ever-new hope in my
heart I entered rich palaces and left them again smitten with ever-
new despair?

Must I tell you what I felt at the advice of the mighty, to make
despair the driving force of my art?

Embrace your despair and sing to us about it, I was advised.

My book of dungeons contains the representation of only the
hundredth part of what was going on in my soul. In those cells my
genius suffered; I gnawed on those chains, forgotten by ungrate-
ful humanity. It was a hellish pleasure for me to dream up martyrs
coming from an embittered heart and to express the suffering of
those spirits in the suffering of their bodies.

Have there ever been more appalling prisons conceived by the
human imagination than my *Carceri*? What other reason than
that of grave guilt could cause an artist to sketch such torture
chambers? And would he not at once have atoned for his deed by
having imposed the most gruesome punishment on himself, more
gruesome than any worldly court could ordain? I depicted the
dungeons that one deserves who commits an outrage out of vanity and envy and jealousy. In those dungeons crime lurks. There
below lie murder and guilt. Morality and understanding and reason count for nothing there. On that terrain of horror and bes-
tiality chaos does not rule, rather—on the contrary—chilling
regularity. Therein lies what is ghastly. That depth and that darkness shield my crime for all time. My life and I myself are no more
than a fog bank of memory, the only memory that deserves to be

conjured up, corrected, and finally beautified. I have committed my crime in radical, suicidal insensibility. I don't want to say any more about that. The punishment fits the crime: to be bereft of all lust for life.

I had understood one thing: Since in Rome, in that depleted center of the world, there were no more contracts for building, I put my immortal vaults and columns on paper and from then on understood all architecture as vision. The sketch is fated to be ruins, the demon of ruins is the sketch. We always take on the spirit of the walls that surround us.

I had to get away from this Rome that enwrapped me like a jail cell, I had to get out into the world in order perhaps to still find a suitable construction site.

I rushed across all of Europe, Asia, and Africa and was transported across the sea, holding fast to the railing, dopey from the wind, twisted with sleeplessness in fart-filled hotel beds. I belong among those people who can basically endure no place on earth and who are happy only between places from which and to which they travel. I am restless, and I know that I have not only wasted my life but even worse have missed out on it. I fight my pathological melancholia nonstop and, in truth, consider myself long since for lost. Often enough I was close to putting an end to my life with my own hands. So I was sitting on the edge of Niagara Falls, but it was frozen over. In Rome I drank rat poison, but it was outdated. In Manila I got hold of a revolver, but it jammed. Between Surabaya and Bandung I almost went down with the plane, but the pilot managed to regain control of it. Railway platform edges and towers attract me magically. For many years I no longer wanted to imagine being able to go on living, for I was unable to see any sense to it, any purpose in living, and whenever I woke up, I was brought down by the vortex of suicidal thoughts that all day and all night never left me. But then I was again and again still too cowardly for suicide. Until now I have had neither the last ounce of strength nor the final determination nor the last strength of character for suicide, however much I tried. But one day, I keep telling myself, I'll do what must be done: I'll commit suicide, because my life and my existence have become meaningless, and the absolute meaninglessness and futility of again and again just going on, and again and again merely extending the intolerability of existence, is senseless.

Sometimes my summer pleasures saved me: to sit on the terrace of a café and at the same time denounce or grumble about whatever turned up in front of me. So I sit there like a vulture whose wings are more in the way than of any use. For hours I can sit on the terrace of a café and damn anything and everything, God and the world outright. Actually, there is hardly a greater pleasure for me than to sit on a summery terrace, watching the people and with cynical generosity to find fault with them and to bitch about them: preferably in Lisbon, in the Café a Brasileira, on the Rua Garrett, next to the bronze Pessoa under the run-down façade of the Hotel Borges. That's a special delicacy in my inconsolable life, for the observer sees through a person whom he observes more ruthlessly and mercilessly than does the one observed see through himself. I take a look at those people and know that each one of them is a story, a book that will never be written. At such moments history seems to exist for itself and not to be concerned about people, although it is made by them. This mad arrogance that I am something better than those I observe satisfies me in a curious way. At such moments I imagine that my art consists only in attacking a human being, that predatory animal, with all the means at my disposal and with him the Creator who should not have produced such a pest.

Meanwhile, I am at times also overcome with the idea of always having just pretended everything to everyone, of having merely acted all my life, of always having merely put on an act and of never having really lived. Then that idea attacks me like a wild animal. So I sit and wait for dawn, but the dawn makes nothing easier. People like us must be alone and abandoned by everyone if they want to do their work. I have no friend. *Friendship:* what a debased word! People mouth it constantly ad nauseam, and they completely disparage it in this way. The word *friendship* has gone downhill as much as the fatally trampled word *love.* But in truth I love my solitude, for I'm not lonesome, and I don't suffer from it. I know very well what I gain by being alone, for I need only look at all the others who don't have such a solitude or know it. There is no friendship. Friends call themselves honest—it's enemies who are, says the philosopher.

I search all over the world for destroyed buildings that I could reconstruct with my creative power, and I applaud storms and earthquakes. For a long time I've tried in vain to control myself, that is, to be the master of my Self. I imagine as a special pleasure the making of myself from my brain outward into a mechanism that can simply be commanded without further ado and that then obeys without further ado. I dream that where reason governs, despair is impossible. But that's only a dream, as I know, for whoever has reason finds everything obscured. The longer I live the more cramped for space my mind becomes. My mind is now already much too cramped. In my ears roars the ever mightier sound of underground eruptions, through my body earthquakes rage, the crash of stonework, the collapse of gigantic walls and towers. Not only do I hear these frightful sounds but I also see and feel them in my much too crowded mind. My brain must endure all these cracks that grow incessantly larger, these breaches, this crumbling, this ripping, this bursting. Again and again it is in my ears. In my mind, which is becoming inexorably more cramped, landslides constantly tumble, and mighty avalanches of boulders. In my too crowded head there is nothing but devastation. Also the walls of my body have become too restricted. And still, and for that reason, I travel in order to take my last step while walking. I hope that every hotel room I enter may be my death chamber.

The colors of the forests around Vancouver intoxicated me. In Beijing I suffocated in the dirt. In Iceland I fed the geysers soft soap to make them boil. On the banks of the Ohio I drank myself senseless. Helsinki's train station sobered me up. Buenos Aires was beguiling—if only there had been no tangos. On Tasmania the cathedral built by convicts in Port Arthur moved me to tears: It was never consecrated because a murderer had laid the altar. Once I sat at night in that church and untied my shoelaces while gulls crashed into beacons. I was reproached incessantly from all sides that I had such ideas at all in an age thoroughly inimical to ideas. All those who had put me out the door, with sounding laughter and shaking heads because they didn't want to believe I would make reality of what I planned, thought I was quite mad. I was declared completely mad, especially by the so-called experts. But that a man with such ideas in his mind can cause confusion among such flatheads by no means proves that this man is crazy, even when the majority of the observers believe that such a man might be crazy, that he must simply be crazy. They listened to me, but they didn't understand me. But mostly they didn't even listen to me. They would have liked nothing better than to remove me from their world. Their art of humiliation has become more and more developed. However, my plans are unique. I have put my entire existence and all my potential at the service of my building plans. And I am firmly convinced that every human being has an idea ultimately fatal to him, one he pursues and that in the end will destroy him.

Living in Europe today is something inhuman. In Europe I had no more air. Having become homeless through my pain, I left what people call the *Old World,* attended by the vague hope that somewhere at the ends of the earth there would be that small safety portal behind the picture out of which one could escape into an ideal house of death. Travel is educational. It stimulates the power of the imagination and is besides a cure for melancholia that comes from being sedentary. Aside from that, I don't care where I am alone. Even the earth turns, stars and planets are in constant motion, not to mention the wind: everything just to show how important it is to keep moving.

And so finally, after my lifelong ailment of reflection, following my sure feeling for mass and volume, I came to Australia, the best place this side of the grave, for with its gigantic red deserts and its outback the fifth continent is the last and largest land with prospects for construction in the world; elsewhere everything is already built up, botched, and spoiled, yes, even destroyed.

I accuse so-called architects, as a group, of the disfigurement and the destruction of the surface of the earth. More and more architects today degenerate into obsequious confectioners of fashionable commodities. So-called architects and all the master builders and construction workers taken together are today nothing but destroyers and defacers of the surface of the earth. With every new construction that they build they commit a new crime against humankind. Every building that is put up today by construction experts is a crime!

The desert of Australia! Last place of hope.

My grandfather had told me already at my cradle about the Franciscan Vincenzo Maria Coronelli, who had the first map of the new continent printed in Venice thirty-two years before my birth and exactly a hundred years before the landing of the first convict prisoners in Sydney Cove. It showed *Nuova Hollanda,* after the Florentine Francesco Berlinghieri and the Venetian Battista Agnese had accomplished corresponding preliminary cartographic work. Suddenly I understood the thirst for travel of my fellow countryman Marco Polo. Venice had always had particular connections with Australia already!

I am a Venetian. I am a Venetian driven by history to extremes. That's the problem—that I come from that pile of manure. Oh, homelands! How can you understand them? When anyone writes about his homeland, his pen resists. My Venetian existence is a farce. Best of all I would like not to belong to any nation. That I am a Venetian is my greatest misfortune. From the beginning Venice was ordained to extinction and chosen for extinction, for the noble city stands on no firm foundation. Its fame grew out of its rotting fish and its rotting walls. Sooner or later Venice will perish, as I will perish sooner or later. Both of us are ideal flops. Inevitably therefore it is my greatest misfortune to be a Venetian.

When I was born, a satanic God drew a black cross over my name. Therefore there is no mercy in my life. From the start I was a fateful creature, and an unlucky star hung over my birth, for I belong to those whose history begins with a heavenly phenomenon. It was the same star under which Dante, Raphael, and Michelangelo were born: Saturn, the black planet of melancholia.

It was my lot from the beginning to spend my life under the thumb of Saturn. Even Aristotle declared that all significant men were and are melancholic. Black gall, then, has a particular effect on character, especially when it is present in excess. It stimulates the power of imagination and promotes genius. Unfathomable Saturn watches over the artist above all. It encourages him to transgress boundaries and at the same time threatens him with downfall and failure. If there is a connection between the seven gifts of the Holy Spirit and the seven planets, then Saturn vouches for the gift of wisdom with the slowness of its orbit and with its gravity, for its essence is speculation. It can be no coincidence that this very gloomy unlucky star belongs to architecture. Whoever is born under Saturn belongs from the beginning to the inconsolable.

I was always old. Old age is ridiculous because it's in the wrong place. Therefore I was born already old because even then I was in the wrong place. With blithe ignorance I entered into the age of failure. Even then I had no reasonable relationship to clock time and calendar time. Time is *in* me as space is *around* me. In old age you remember everything, as you do at birth—and understand nothing. You know only one thing: Life will be one single sequence of defeats. Therefore old age is just, for in old age life lies very close to its negation, as it does at birth. And I was always different from everything else and everyone else. And I was different with each one, so that to this very day no one really knows how I was. From the start I knew that I had to set out in a different direction than the others, take a different path than the others, live a different life than the others. With that, something had begun that could not be reversed by anything anymore. Why did I also have to see the colossal buildings of Venice about me in my infancy?

My whole life is just one big disaster. Life: What stupidity to have to suffer under that measly light. The light for which I yearn extinguishes the stars. That's why they said about me later that the most difficult thing to resist about my pictures was the mysterious, mildly solemn light that falls from the side or from above over the vault. It augured forgetting—and a different kind of peace.

But having been born, humankind learns the dread of a bottomless well shaft. Before you so easily say that life is the highest of all good things, calmly compare the sum of all conceivable joys that a man can enjoy in his life with the sum of every possible suffering that can strike him in his life. *Mille piacer'non vagliono un tormento:* A thousand pleasures are not worth one torment.

I am involuntarily a human being. The crime of having been born cannot be forgiven. As the purpose of our existence we can mention nothing more than the recognition that we would be better off not being here. Our whole being, including the unbearable hieroglyphs such as happiness, love, joy, is something that were better not in existence, since the world is in no way prepared for it. Such a thing brings nothing but misfortune. Beware of building the so-called happiness of your being on a broad foundation, for that is where it is most likely to collapse. Happiness consists at best of living more with books than with people. I have always taken shelter in books as though on an island. Books always intervened in history. To this very day they count among the archives and the laboratories of our perception of the world as well as of the perception of ourselves. In them are kept hopes as well as contradictions on which those hopes are shattered. And even freedom has nested frequently first and last between the letters of the alphabet. Nobility exists only in the negation of being, says the philosopher. We reproduce like the birds and the bees and yet can't fly. Later I believed that only death could eradicate this misfortune. But death did not come for me. From that you can appreciate what a misfortune it is for me not to be able to die. I cannot die for just one reason, because in certain situations I can bring my heart to a standstill just as I can my rational thought. That's like plunging through a looking glass. The corpse in me can do that. Death is not a folding smokescreen between the living, as the poet sings. You see, death is nothing but a frightful misunderstanding. In this it resembles the frightful misunderstanding that puts us into the world. We are put into a world that consists only of nothing but frightful misunderstandings and that we can endure only as a frightful misunderstanding because we leave it again with a frightful misunderstanding, for after birth death is the greatest and most frightful misunderstanding of all, for which I am the living example. The beyond keeps sending us its dead.

What are all the efforts of humankind in comparison with the futile and ridiculous attempt to resist the phenomenon of death by trying to make sense of it, as though you could give it any other meaning than the one it has?

Failure is a condition of life. Man cannot escape that because he can free himself from nothing at all, for only in the moment of his death does he leave the dungeon into which he is begotten. We enter a world that is supposed to be for us but is not at all prepared for us, and we must come to terms with that world. If we don't come to terms with it, then we perish. Ninety-nine percent of human beings, of course, when they have died, have lived only in the world supposed to be for them, but not ever in their own.

I have understood that from the beginning. Also that I should never have been allowed to be born. There are so many so-called human beings who should never have been allowed to be born. Therefore you have to treat them gently.

I was innately talented, but what am I saying—now it's already too late to deny it—I came into the world as a very uncommon genius and yet am and remain a living protest against the ridiculous idea of a superman. To be more precise, I came seemingly dead and ancient into the world, lit by a full moon in the tracks of which I have since walked. The day before, my mother had felt a great desire for crabs. The midwife grabbed my little legs with a stranglehold, held me head down, and gave me the customary slap. But I didn't react. There was some talk about what to do. At first they wrapped me in damp cloths, finally laid me in ice-cold water. My parents already thought they had to despair of me, for I still hadn't made a sound. Then a gravedigger coming by chance along the way whirled me several times through the air like a club, tucked me in diapers, and shoved me in the preheated stovepipe where I began to cry pitifully. Thirty-two years later in far-away Bristol a child prodigy is said to have been brought to life in a similar manner. Since then I know that I will never ever escape myself.

One of my earliest memories: I was standing in the corner of a room, bent over to the wall, propping my head and staring at the blood that was flowing abundantly from my nose and dripping onto the floor. I was crying for my mother. She had gone into another room to weep. Frightened by the nosebleed, my grandmother took the lad to a witch in Murano for me to undergo a remarkable hocus-pocus and to inform me of a visit by a lovely woman in the coming night. When I woke up a few hours later, I saw a beautiful woman wrapped in a hoop skirt and veiled in dazzling material coming down the chimney to me. On her head she wore a crown strewn with gems from which sparks flew. Slowly and majestically the woman stepped nearer and sat down on my bed. She took some small boxes from her pocket, emptied them on my head, and murmured strange words. Then she made me a long speech, of which I understood not a word, kissed me on my brow, and disappeared just as mysteriously as she had come.

My father, Angelo, whose family came from Pirano in Istria, where the white limestone of Venetian palaces was quarried, was a stonecutter and with his handiwork had acquired such prestige that he was able to marry Laura Lucchesi, the older sister of a respected engineer and architect, and thus could move into the better society of Venice. Anyway, my godfather was Giovanni Widmann, who belonged to one of the richest families of the Serenissima. But the bent to art of my family's social class was initially strange, since it had practiced mainly in the proficiency of service. Inherited from my father was my anxiety, which I cursed and fought against with the total expenditure of my willpower, anxiety that befalls me for the slightest reason with such force at times that I see only possible, hardly conceivable misfortune incarnate before me. A terrible fantasy at times heightens this unhappy predisposition into the incredible. So in the first years of my life I was already seized by the misery of life like Buddha in his youth, when he saw sickness, old age, pain, and death. From my childhood on, the passion for architecture developed in me. When I think back on that time, I smell the drawing pen, the aroma sweet and woody. On a board on the shelf over the oven stood the words:

> *All the teardrops of your lifetime*
> *trickle through a cellar crack.*
> *Do not cry, for it is futile:*
> *A whip will still land on your back.*

That should have been a warning to me, but I paid no attention to the saying. But from the beginning I groveled. Once as a child I bloodied my knee and waited for Death to crawl in through the wound. He is still on his way. My left shoulder droops only because Death is constantly squatting on it, directly over my heart, like a parrot on a pirate's shoulder. There Death squats, presses me down, and still doesn't come.

Because of my extraordinary drawing talent, my father decided I would become an architect and sent me as an apprentice to my father-in-law Matteo Lucchesi, who was responsible for the improvement and upkeep of the mighty seawalls protecting the Venetian lagoon.

While I was learning the rules of Palladio from Matteo, my older brother Angelo, a Carthusian monk, was lecturing me evening after evening about the most important events in Roman history, taught me the Latin language, and with his tales of the legendary heroic deeds of the ancient Romans kindled the fire of my imagination. Only in the imagination does every truth find an effective and irrefutable existence. A modest library, which had an odor of apples and wood, opened up for me a boundless world of iridescent fantasy. My earliest dreams became visions in which the simple surroundings of my childhood paled. If you experience historical information in your imagination, truth can become reality. Otherwise, my childhood, that ridiculous epoch of picking your nose, consisted of nothing but dreadful things.

Reading to myself and reading aloud determined my life. Many a book went off like the thunder of cannon. Among my favorite things to read was also the *Favole* of Leonardo da Vinci.

I read a lot, and whenever I was reading, the words seemed to open like oysters to show me their most intimate meaning. At night I dreamed of battles and Caesars and was gripped by a wild passion to travel to Rome to see the famous memorials, where so many mighty deeds had taken place, but above all to sketch the monuments that to this day bear witness to those things. When this Rome had engulfed me, it was as though I had heard myself. For me it was a high-altitude flight. You can't measure the height of the flight by the extent of the fall. Sometimes I thought that the shock of the world was there only to take me to Rome. I looked, it was said of me, as though I could see through walls. Yet I was often dejected and as mute as a fish. And I was so thin that I could fit between a door and its hinges.

One thing I knew, no, that I already had a presentiment of then: A giant was within me. But that giant was still in chains. Besides, he was lonely, as only children and old people can be lonely. Even back then I realized that I would have to come to terms with that, for an artistic person cannot be with others at all for long.

I was borne along by the idea that there must be more than all of that. At the age of three I developed a personal dot technique, and already a year later I began to draw objects in perspective: a nicely shortened side wall, a tree shrunken by distance, a jug that half hid a glass. Shortly afterward I discovered the tints of shadows and with that the difference between the shadow of an apple and that of a plum. I studied and improved my possibilities of expression with the care and devotion of a curious child. As a six-year-old with an incorruptible eye for satanic traps I tried to paint air the color of urine and fever, as though even then I had a presentiment that my life would be an incessant battle with irrational things that had plotted against me.

But my eyes could learn to see only in darkness.

In my daydreams I sketched Rome as the world empire of architecture. Concerning that, and because the next day I seldom had enough sleep but to make up for it was all the more hot tempered, I soon got into an argument with my uncle, and after fierce quarrels, cursing like a coachman and howling my head off, I left his workshop in order to enter the atelier of Carlo Zucchi, who had made a name for himself as teacher of perspective, stage designer, graphic artist, and engraver.

Learning required no effort of me. Often enough it even went too slowly for me. I was so furiously young. Once I gave my godfather a drawing and wrote on it: *Guard this sheet, which doubtless will become very valuable when I get to be famous.*

From the start, drawing was for me the only possibility of survival. My drawing was the memory of a destruction that at the same time was the destruction of a memory. Besides, as my contemporary Diderot wrote in his *Essay on Painting,* you should mistrust any architect who cannot draw: *How can that man otherwise have taught his eye? Where should he have gotten the particularly fine feeling for proportions? Where should he otherwise have acquired his ideas about grandeur and simplicity?*

I owe the study of perspective and practice with the etching needle, above all the agility to create splendid, superdimensional structures, to that period of uneasiness and restlessness. Society's passion for the theater of the time opened up for architects an inexhaustible field of activity. They were responsible for ever more daring constructions of space, every more grandiose decorations for festivals, ever more magnificent processions. In addition, Zucchi taught me a certain pedantry that is necessary for the perfection of technical skills.

When after the death of the old Clement XII the election of his successor was about to take place, in February 1740 the Signoria dispatched a new ambassador to Rome. Through all kinds of bowing and scraping, but also on the basis of my talent, I got myself assigned to him as a graphic artist. I passionately believed that with that I had climbed the first rung of my unstoppable career as an architect, and deep inside I knew that that ladder would lead me to immortality. I believed it with a lightheartedness that I later lost, and I felt more exalted than the ambassador, for my visions, all of which were still slumbering in me and waiting only to be awakened, lifted me above all of those who saw only the gifted graphic artist in me. It wouldn't be long until they had to recognize whom they had at their side. I wanted to show everyone what I could do and what I had inside of me—everyone.

With burning ambition.

From that moment on, at the latest, I was transformed into a workhorse.

To hide my excessively touchy feelings and my exaggerated sensitivity, I withdrew behind a façade of haughty arrogance, kept myself apart, and seldom spoke to anyone. Although hardly anyone knew me, I enjoyed making myself unknowable. That I had grown a beard fit in with this attitude. That gave me the appearance of a nobleman. I, with my bearded hawk face and the proud brilliance of my dream! Caesar and Augustus had gone beardless. Only since Hadrian had wearing a beard come into fashion.

But a beard doesn't make a philosopher. *Ed io anche son pittore.* That is: Architecture denies its exclusive character of purpose and should be judged in accordance with aesthetic viewpoints. The neglect of a practical useful value makes possible the departure from spatial and constructive logic and the organization of structural integrity solely through factors of effectiveness. With that, architecture is no longer bound by criteria of construction but depends much more on principles of design, with which the visual arts are acquainted: It becomes artistic architecture. Architecture becomes art! With that, historical art becomes citable in my ideal of *varietà*. At the same time this confirms the architect as the *master builder of the world*. To me architecture is not only the object of a picture, rather the picture is also an accomplishment of architecture. An aesthetic world order is always simultaneously the illustration of history.

Art, as I found out, performs in passing the task of conserving, also of retouching dimmed, faded ideas a bit; when it has accomplished that task, it weaves a bond with various epochs and makes their spirits return.

In this sense, exactly at the time of my reckless as well as criminal conception, Fischer von Erlach wrote his *Plan of a Historical Architecture* and sums up a three-thousand-year-old history of form. In the end there is no longer reconstruction to restore the form of antiquity, rather there is reproduction to herald that and other exemplary characteristics. For me antiquity creates the opportunity to legitimize my own art in its historical position and to see it in a series with ancient architecture and derive it from that. Thus ancient art largely loses its transtemporal-ideal character. This explains my glorification of Roman architecture. Admittedly, I do not form a chronological series but exemplary architectural situations. I understand the results of the history of architecture up to now as a treasure trove of form out of which my *inventio* derives. I deal with architecture in a completely new way and in doing so distance myself from the solutions that were known at the time, and clearly contradict the normed canon as it is expressed in the Vitruvian rules.

The encounter with the *ruine parlanti* of Rome led me to an idea of antiquity and architecture that has nothing in common with a reconstruction that aims simply at a revival of ancient form.

I undertook my explorations from my quarters in the Palazzo Venezia at the upper end of the Via del Corso. With restless energy and hectic impatience I sought to fathom the mystery of the ancient ruins, studied and sketched the fields of rubble on site—now alone, now in the company of a fellow countryman, the sculptor Corradini, so that then during the nights I could continue to finish my notes under the mocking glow of the stars. The consequence was a physical and mental breakdown that tied me to my feverish bed for weeks. It was to me as though a demonic swarm of hornets were piercing me. Madness enveloped me like a golden cloud. In those hours I became a stone eater. They put compresses on me, bled me briefly because of such a feverish chest ailment, and it seemed to me as though my breath were slowly drawn out and a strange, hotter one blown into me. However, I felt these fantasies that drenched my bedding not only as painful but also as highly enjoyable and stimulating. After all, they held up images to my eyes that I soon wanted to transform into stone.

To cure me of my obsession I worked for the brothers Domenico and Giuseppe Valeriani on theatrical scenery and festival decorations. I sat in with the architect Salvi, who completed the Fontana di Trevi, and in order to perfect my etching technique apprenticed myself to Giuseppe Vasi. At times I wanted to hang up architecture completely and apply myself to painting, which my friends from the French Academy encouraged me to do. To gain clarity, again to become calm inwardly so that a decision could be reached, I traveled to Naples. But the etching needle wouldn't turn me loose. Incessantly it touched ultimate things. It is even more merciless than invisible thought because it has that degree of toughness that bears endurance and survival within itself.

All the attempts to shake off my solitude failed even at the start. I wrote hundreds of letters to all kinds of people to get into contact with them, but I didn't even send off all those letters. Rather, I piled them up in the chests in which I had also locked away all my portfolios with my impracticable plans. Even while writing the letters I realized the impossibility of letting them be delivered. I constantly had the desire to make contacts, but my powers disappeared even more with each new attempt. In addition came the meanness and malice and insidiousness of people around me who were interested only in money, eating, drinking, and whoring, people who more and more and in all their manifestations gathered together with the sole purpose of destroying me and obliterating me entirely, against which I was powerless and without any protection. Everywhere I see mindlessness, greed, and hypocrisy at work; brutality and baseness alone prevail now.

And the scornful laughter of those who despise me pursues me to this very day and remains for me a frightful abyss. They had money for everything—any senseless ostentation, any nonsense, any empty carousing, any kind of saber rattling was supported, not to mention the courtesans who devoured millions.

They wanted to do nothing for only one man: for me.

As soon as I spread out my plans, I was always involved only with cowardly civil servants, with shabby subordinates, with piteous professors. Today all over the world only dull mediocrity is accepted and determines what is built and what isn't.

It's a shame, a crime, a scandal.

Even Nature is against me. Proof of that is death, which is also against me by refusing me.

How gladly I would have left this barbarity called life behind me at the right time. Again and again I wish I were long since dead, but then I discover that I'm still alive or again that I'm not dead. I'm alive, and the days pass by, soundlessly, hot, heavy, sinking one after the other into the past as though into a chasm. The past directs the future like an orchestra deliberately playing out of tune. Crushingly the rings of my years wrap around my heart. The impossible always takes a little longer. The past is in reality always a *lostness*. What has been and is no more is just as non-existent as what never was. And everything that is, in the next instant has been. There is only the present dwindling away. But letting the past be shrugged off, leaving the future to providence—both of those mean not to understand the significance of the present, which can be valid as reality only when it can preserve the past through loyalty to memory, when it understands how to assimilate the future through the consciousness of responsibility. Of course, in the end everyone runs aground shipwrecked and without masts, and so, then, life is nothing but a Saint Vitus' dance into the arms of death, made a fool of by hope. But death has up to now always only said no to me.

No.

How often have I heard that, that omni-destructive *No*. I stepped up to my audience, but no one had come. Without having made my entrance, I had to withdraw. Everything I did was futile, but what is futile must be done. That makes art invulnerable. Art serves no one. It is a fact, not a commentary. Not a line on the copperplate that would not be flesh. And art must always be the destroyer of today in the name of what is to come. You can't just want art but must wait with no way out until it intrudes upon you. In general, all art borders on the ridiculous, on defeat, and on humiliation. Art trusts the virtues of the unlucky. Building is for an architect nothing more than an eternal battle that the artist fights with the rest of humankind for his outstanding significance.

Besides, I became stronger than any fate because with every stroke of my pen I dared the futile anew. I used every possible trick unworthy of a genius—flattery and kowtowing—but in vain!

In vain.

Invano.

After three years of frantic work I published my first independent cycle of etchings, a series of twelve sheets with fantasy structures. And for them I wrote a dedication to the Roman builder Nicola Giobbe, in which I emphasized that marvelous ruins were still the most perfect things that architecture had produced in its stern majesty and from the Roman spirit of grandeur: *I just want to report,* I wrote, *that these speaking ruins have filled my mind with images that exact drawings, even those of the immortal Palladio, can never rouse, although I have always held them up before me. That's why the wish rose within me to reveal some of these images to the world. But since, at the same time, no architect of today can hope to execute even a single one of them (whether that is the fault of architecture itself, which has fallen away from the blessed perfection that it had achieved in the greatest age of the Republic and the strongest emperors who then followed—or whether of the people who would have been obligated to support this most elegant of our powers of creation as patrons): in any case, since in our day neither do structures come into being nor do princes or private citizens show any inclination to have such things come into being—then I see no other way for myself or any*

*other modern architect than to announce my own ideas through
sketches in order to overtake the lead that sculpture and painting enjoy
in regard to architecture; and in order at the same time to remove architecture from the despotism of those who have great wealth and
therefore believe they can decree its goals and efforts as they see fit. For
no other reason have I worked to add my own knowledge of architecture, however it may be judged, to the other art: not only to draw my
inspirations but also to put them on copperplate.*

Ruins were always the realm where architecture and Nature
met most clearly. *Follow the owl,* says a proverb from the Magreb,
and it will lead you to a ruin. The owl is the symbol of wisdom:
Ergo, wisdom leads to ruins. Art historians say that ruins are bear-
ers of sentiment and that architectural ruins are intent on effect.
Even the darkness, the crumbling, mauled majesty of the structure, the mute echo elicit our humble respect.

Fantasy, *inventio,* and *varietà* can be especially well demonstrated with ruins. In that regard, the ruin-form is the beginning
state, not the final state. From this comes the paradox that the
greatest possible effect of architecture is to be gained only in
something like that, which can no longer be achieved as the consequence of decay and the destruction of its original purpose. Up
to now the concept of ruin was principally linked to historical
buildings. Now, on the basis of melancholy in the face of earthly
transitoriness, it becomes an icon of vanitas and thus of poetry.
The idea of architecture is realized only in ruins. Ruins evoke sublime feelings in me. Wandering among ruins means to me to be
wandering through eternities. Wherever I look, the objects everywhere surrounding me point to the end of all things. So I also
come to terms with the end that awaits me. You have to let a
palace collapse in order to make an object of interest out of it.

Even an ugly construction can gain through demolition. Its parts can be jumbled up fantastically, apart from the fact that the destruction of the ugly creates a certain satisfaction. That a ruin can appear to be beautiful is determined not only by the original construction and the manner of its destruction but also by whether the building becomes one with surrounding Nature and it even takes on the character of a natural work. With roof and window and door being open, with all isolation set aside, with moss turning the ashlar green, plants rooting between the stones, birds building their nests, and everything covered with weeds, the structure has in effect become a creation of Nature that buries all *joie de vivre* anyway because ruin is the essential substance of Nature.

A new world had arisen before my eyes: the fantastic dream of an infinity of architecture that has its origin in the sublimity of ancient Rome and at the same time is able to draw the appropriate picture of that lost grandeur only in its unfettered arbitrariness of invention.

Columned halls and temples, sweeping staircases and magnificent bridges: Components of a forum for an imaginary world empire were the result. My journeyman's piece of such Baroque theatrical sets, wavering still between painting and architecture, served me as groundwork for the later prison scenes. I got additional polish and a few impulses from the old Ferdinando Galli Bibiena in Bologna, whose stage architecture was obligated only to his own idea and, already for quite some time, no longer to the staged weak plays or even to the dubious taste of the audience, which constantly craved something new.

Even back then I had to hear the reproach that my architecture could no longer be built, that I was striving to overpower the observer. Yet I was really intent on pulling him into the picture.

To do that I made use of various tricks: the tilting of the point of view, the bizarre breakdown of the walls and arcades, the round and triangular gables as well as the decisive trick of the corner point, in order to cut out a smaller space by means of the walls or the order of columns running to the rear from the left and right diagonally to a point of intersection, from which I then could organize the perspective anew. I preferred to have the onlooker see through side rooms into a main room and thus remove the peepshow aspect. The endless series of galleries and staircases spread out into a labyrinth that seemed to have only corridor rooms but no center. Grasses, branches, blossoms, and trees crowded around collapsed ruins that reared up for me into a strange and dwarfish present as mysterious monuments of unknown greatness and guilt: for the glory of forgotten heroes and vanished triumphs. From that arises my basic tone of mourning, because I felt that only pathetic admiration in the form of a copy—but no longer the power for new and artistically independent construction—had remained for my own time.

That also applied directly to me, for all my life I have always been an admirer. Today I know what was wrong in that regard: The state of admiration is a condition of feeblemindedness. Most people are feebleminded all their lives only because they admire. Only a dimwit admires, the smart one doesn't admire: he respects, observes, understands.

That's the difference!

By my apparently paying tribute to megalomania, I have in reality merely relativized grandeur. Great architecture tells no story, rather it is the result of a recognition that words cannot replace. Where they can do so, it is not great architecture. But the mightier the vision an artist has, the more he must make it reality in his art. Aside from that, the Italian language tends to the superlative anyway. As soon as it expresses enthusiasm, it calls something not only fabulous or beautiful but at the same time cries out *bravissimo*... What happens then, when an Italian speaks? He never knows whether a word is good enough or not. So what does he do? He emphasizes every word with his hands, with greater and greater movements, with his whole body. All who listen to him stare as though spellbound at his hands that dance wildly around him like birds in a nosedive. But hardly does he put his hands in his pockets than his words also stick in his throat. He can't think of a single one. In desperation he tears his hands out of his pockets and spreads them in great gestures of regret. A new opera begins.

The end of Foscarini's ambassadorship forced me to leave Rome again in the spring of 1744 and to return to Venice because of a lack of funds. The realization of having to be, like a slave, dependent for money and favor on influential personalities was extremely painful.

I hoped for a building contract—in vain.

In vain: Again I heard the main phrase of my life. For naught, in vain, *invano.* My life stretches between them, and I can still dream only of shadows.

So I increasingly developed as an expert in futility, in the jaws of which I became more and more entangled, whose stranglehold I feel to this very day. Sometimes I succeed in deadening and minimizing this awareness of futility, but as soon as I feel the iron collar again, I could in furious helplessness bash my skull against the nearest wall.

In me burned the ambition to become the chronicler of Rome's antiquity, at least as a graphic artist—the excavations of Herculaneum had made an enormous impression upon me. So I immersed myself in the secrets of the Venetian art of etching and scenic painting in the studio of Giambattista Tiepolo.

In my *Capriccio* I tried to combine dizzying perspective and melancholy. The play with horror, the ambiguity of gesture and mimicry, the magic midday aura of Pan and death in Arcadia were to flow into one another. Impermanence became my dominant theme. Decline and endurance, the inevitability of perishing in becoming busied me as thoughts, but at every step behind every ivy-covered wall I met the world of antiquity—abandoned columns and gods in banishment. Only Goya was to succeed in something equivalent with his *Caprichos*.

Just a year after my return to my homeland I settled again in Rome as the agent of the Venetian graphic artist and art dealer Giuseppe Wagner. I set myself up in the Via del Corso, opposite the Palazzo Mancini, the seat of the French Academy.

During that time I created those four *Grotteschi*, which the interpreters of all times were to tackle in vain—after all, they contain metaphors and symbols of long-since forgotten occult doctrines of the Pythagoreans and Neoplatonists, of alchemy and Oriental mythology. Besides, they make good on my responsibilities, which as a member of the Roman Academy of Arcadias— under the shepherd's name of Salcindio Tiseio—as well as a secret member of a Freemason lodge, I had agreed to. My *Grotteschi* are poems without words on the themes of vanitas and melancholia. Anyone who is amazed at winged monsters and stranded dolphins on a garden wall has no need to first ask about the solution of the riddle.

In the same year Rousseau published his *Discours sur les sciences et les arts*, and Goldoni brought my favorite fairy tale, the land of Cockaigne, to the stage of our father city, whose audience was able to admire the piece *Il Paese di Cuccagna* in the Teatro Giustinian di S. Mosè on Ascension Day in 1750. Also in Rome and Bologna they celebrated the *Cuccagna del porco;* it was surpassed only by the *Cuccagna Napoletana:* wagons provisioned with food-stuffs that were drawn in triumph through the city, accompanied by dancing, costumed people, until they fell victim to general plundering regularly, but especially in the year of starvation, 1764, which turned into butchery, injury, and death. Saturday, the 11th of February, remained memorable. Instead of the carts they had erected a house of wood that was decorated with bread, sausages, fresh meat, live steers and cows, with lambs, dried cod, and other foodstuffs. At the signal of a cannon shot, the house was plundered, whereby the whole city fell into stark turmoil. There was tumult and loud screaming, so that the opera, which was being held in the Royal Theater, had to be stopped, for those of the public armed with swords ran off and started a bloody skirmish with the cavalry.

Say yes or say no—you must dance though.

That's how the dance of death goes that I learned on my one trip into the north over the Alps. In traveling, you heap life on life, says the philosopher. I idolized what was savage and primeval, while approaching it in comfort. My way led as far as Birg, where I left my tracks behind me. I rode with a postal inspector, who gave me the advice never to marry. In the end I had to promise him with a handshake, and so we parted as good friends. In the shop of the baker Anastasius Aschkring there hangs an etching that depicts the bakery vault with its Gothic ribs, fantastically extended and peopled with mysterious shapes.

You will wonder how it happens that I gave one of my etchings to a baker in a godforsaken dump named Birg. It was out of gratitude, for Master Aschkring taught me an old folk song that seemed to me to be a melody to my own life gone wrong:

When I sit at my spinning wheel
and twist my thread to sew:
There stands a little hunchback there
who won't let the wheel go.

A little hunchback!
La panetteria di Birghi.
Anyway, Birg and its sayings!

Dying wives won't give you hives,
But a stallion's death will steal your breath.

Later, art historians couldn't believe that I had ever come through Birg, but how can you depend on art historians? They can always only interpret, since they themselves have created nothing. They didn't even recognize the influence of Rembrandt upon my etching technique.

But anyone who has built a world as I have doesn't have to interpret it.

Art historians have formed an impression of me. Where once the idea was important, today it's the image. The image is stronger than the reality that it determines, and the devil with ideas. Ideas are a part of history, while the dominance of image begins where history ends. Today image dictates our behavior, political viewpoints, as well as aesthetic tastes. It may be different tomorrow. The human being becomes his image, over which he no longer has control. And we can do nothing, absolutely nothing, about the image that others have of us. It's a mystery to us. And who is constantly at work to construct an image of every artist? Critics and art historians. The crime of critics and art historians consists not of starting with the question of whether the artist has been successful in doing what he wished but of passing judgment about what in their opinion he should have done.

Therefore art historians and art critics are the real destroyers of art, as a spiritual brother once said, also one damned and possessed, who worked constantly on the wheel of history, on his world piece. I don't know now in which century that was, but it's of no matter, for it's still valid. This buffoon of despair is close to my heart as hardly any other is. He was a grandiose wrecker, who never grew weary of spitting his embitterment and his demolitions in uncouth and deeply hateful infinite loops into the face of the world until it was totally obliterated, disguised now as blathering, then again as grumbling or as niggling, but always with unequaled fervor in a tirade, which was his preferred form. His words have meanwhile become flesh and blood to me, especially since, as a lover of ruins, I am in fact an admirer of wreckage. To every statement he has left, I would like to scream *yes* at the top of my voice, as though he had foreseen me and my ridiculous, miserable life gone wrong along with its tormentors.

Critics, he said, if I remember correctly, prattle on about art until they have prattled it to death. The business of the critic was the nastiest business in existence, and a prattling critic—and there were only prattling critics—should be chased out of the art world with an ox pizzle. We should not let our art be destroyed by critics. If we listened to a critic, said the inventor of the wheel of history, we would fall ill; by listening to a critic, we would see how the art that he prattled about is destroyed. This absolutely revolting and disgusting intercourse of the race of critics, this critic art prattle, this critic cock-a-doodle-*dumb* that is loved on all sides, has always revolted me. Once the good Lord had a marvelous idea, and HE created the artist. But then came the Devil and had a much better idea. He created the critic.

The unwavering arrogance of the human being makes itself felt especially with the critic. There someone cries out in despair, and the critic stands by and examines whether he has hit the right note. Just imagine for a moment the following scene: A human being paints an animal on the stone wall of the Caves of Lascaux. Someone stands behind him, peers over his shoulder, and says: The front legs are too short. Putting up with critics is a constant in every artist's life, in every one.

Recently art historians, those deplorable derivatives of critics, have asserted impudently that in reality I wasn't concerned about building at all, that a constructed realization of my graphic depictions was not at all intended and was out of the question from the start, for the realization of my architecture was already present in the picture. Art historians even go so far as the unheard-of lie that especially my *Carceri* derogates architecture merely as a means to an end, as staff and background. And yet those hallways are so deep and those walls so thick that no mockery by critics can destroy them. Those dungeons depict a world in which everything has become architecture. There is no outside any longer within those spaces, only an inside. The world of the *Carceri* is an interior world. Its darkness serves as illumination, for light is not always suitable for letting things be seen better.

La panetteria di Birghi: Here you can make a lot of observations that are transformed from raw law into frost and cold. A gloomy, doubly cerebral solitude prevails. Don't look for Birg on any map;

real places are never there. All the places in the world weigh down upon Birg. Birg: not suitable for marginal notes.

Art historians and critics were of the opinion that *La panetteria di Birghi* was counterfeit. But everything in Birg is false, so it's not a counterfeit, it belongs. As you no doubt know, the empress Catherine once came to the Crimea and wanted to visit a village that had presumably been built there for the poor. But it did not exist. They built a dummy city, the empress drove fast as the wind through the dummy street. But I was in Birg. I saw the dance of death. And since my visit to the area of Birg the idea of the dance of death has also guided my cold needle. *Entrance of Death in a Whirl of Confetti*. With that statement everything began.

As far as the imaginary prisons are concerned—the dark dungeons with their iron rings and their winches, the gloomy torture chambers—they are familiar to me firsthand from my homeland as well as from my visit to even gloomier Birg. Everyone knows about the horrors of the Venetian lead chambers, the prison cells of the Roman Mount Angelus, or the mamertine dungeons under the Church of San Giuseppe dei Falegnami. With every official palace, whether it be that of the doges or the one on the Capitol, whether I want to or not, I involuntarily see the dungeons connected with it. No power can manage without dungeons. Besides, in the first place it is not a matter of the reality of such prisons, rather the idea of them that I wanted to convey to my contemporaries: The dungeon as a mirror of the world, distorted and exaggerated, but in that way all the truer—the dungeon as a terrible counterworld in which our terrible world can be depicted. It's as though a theater director intentionally staged his own play as an unsuccessful production: a statement that my critics, eager for my slaughter, can put forward at any time against me. All the same, these prisons would have to be gloomy and awaken in the observer the idea that he himself was standing in a vault situated deep under the surface, doomed to an inescapable imprisonment.

More and more, my own ideas were caught in the vortex of an infinity walled into a dungeon. The wooden roof timbers, the clumsily built ashlars, the ladders and shoddy balustrades of balconies as well as the endless arches of arcades are nothing more than an expression of my dream visions that surged toward me at a bewildering speed: the result perhaps of that infection that I caught on my passages through the marshes of the Campagna before Rome. Again and again the fever attacked me, again and again it threw me onto my cot, sent me into a miserable state of pitiable helplessness—and yet I owed ever-new visions to it. These were accompanied by shortness of breath, dizziness, pounding heart, an oppressive feeling, pestilential flatulence, and painful erections with a cold sweat. I slept lighter than a bird. In such hours I succumbed to the idea that all the buildings of Rome were transparent. I saw from the attics under the roof timbers down to the catacombs; I saw the half-dark hallways and corridors; I saw into the cellar holes and niches, into secret passageways as well as into elegant sleeping chambers where desire was clad in silk. And naked scorn grinned at me from every side. In this way I learned to pray to the fever, even to crave it. Thomas De Quincey, a Romantic opium eater, later spread the viewpoint that I, too, had tried that poison. What touching English nonsense. It was the strange Piranesi fever, not opium!

I battled my high blood pressure with leeches, little creatures that reminded you of Hell, born only to suck out black blood. I put them behind my ears and drained them then when, full of blood, they fell off by themselves. Fished out of the wild brooks in the area, they were offered for sale in cork-sealed clay containers by hawkers. And I was a good customer.

Just don't believe that at my work I would have disregarded the observers of my art.

On the contrary!

The observer always lingers on the inside of these dungeons. And since I was always the first observer of my visions, I felt shoved into these monstrous prisons, my gaze turned directly upward, before my eyes the covered arches and spatial shafts, the immeasurability of abandonment in infinity, obstructed by shadowy bridges and staircases from the interstices that have no identifiable connection any longer to one another, made a fool of by the deliberately confused motifs reflected in silvery brightness that fell from the side naves and that even in the stories located deepest gave a suggestion of the reflection of new sources of light. Then the towers and walls faded into the inchoate background cross-hatching, while the openings of the arches pushed into one another inexorably. Clouds of fog and mist made breathing difficult for me. Harassed thus, I transferred the dream visions that I persistently received from my fever onto the plate so that my etching needle was hardly able to follow my rushing anxiety. The dream disturbed the reality of the day I had lived through. Therein it resembles art.

Unsociable and possessed by my work in equal measure, I looked for a confidant and publisher who would keep bothersome visitors and creditors off my neck, disseminate my work, and otherwise be dependable. I yearned for a person whom I could trust, who understood me, and who followed me unconditionally. And I knew that a woman would never be up to such requirements. I did not despise women as such but did despise their idolatry and their unimpeded position of privilege. I found such a person in Jean Bouchard, a well-read bookdealer near the Church of S. Marcello on the Via del Corso. He belonged to that French colony of artists that I had been acquainted with since my first sojourn in Rome. Bouchard's printing house lay not far from the rooms in which I had set up my workshop: right across from the French Academy in the Palazzo Mancini.

After my *Carceri* had found neither an echo nor understanding among my contemporaries, I changed over—harking to necessity as well as to the command of the hour—to views for the glorification of Rome. Instead of realizing my dreams as a master architect, I had to open up a shop in order to keep myself tenaciously above water as an engraver and art dealer. Just imagine: a shop! How I loathed this shopkeeping. On the one hand it made a livelihood possible and in that regard was welcome, but on the other hand I felt like a bound man. That art photographer who lived from the postcard of the cursed sunset on Capri must later not have felt otherwise.

Making a virtue out of necessity, I agreed to a collaboration with Carlo Nolli. It concerned a continuation of the work of his father along with a smaller version of *Nuova Pianta di Roma*. My task consisted not only in contributing an architectural *pasticcio* to the new city map but also in participating in wearisome and time-consuming research and reexamination—after all, it was a matter of nothing less than the fantastic restoration of ancient Rome at the time of the Caesars. For ten years—in the case of my plan for Hadrian's Villa—I worked as a would-be city planner, as they would describe it today, on these ground plans. And it was all only pretend architecture, because the unspeakable powers that be, foremost the princes of the Church, virtually suffocating with their riches, sought nothing but extravagant development in order to set up a monument in stone for themselves for eternity. At the same time they carelessly allowed the preserved temples of antiquity to fall into dilapidation and made use of them at best as quarries and dumping grounds.

All that remained for me were small views of Rome in quarto format. Admittedly, they soon sold like hotcakes. I pocketed my share and laid it aside carefully for my views. But what a pathetic job, preparing illustrations for a travel guide, the great skill of which—say, in their bright-dark composition—was not even recognized, much less treasured.

Do you even know what architecture is? The art of building is not only the portrait of an epoch but a treatise on Being, a survey, an encyclopedia of life: *Exemplum de quodam homine, qui volebat aedificare domum* . . . Architecture is a highly philosophical art, but so-called builders have never grasped that. For that reason we are almost never involved with the art of building but with building what is shoddy. Building borders on the miraculous. Everyone has the desire to build, but not everyone has also the possibility, of which I myself am the best proof. Only building could redeem me. Of course, only an architectural work that has never before been built affords the highest satisfaction. But in the end, when such an architectural work is finished, nothing but a great shock awaits it.

The history of architecture must be written the other way around, that is, as the history of what was not built. Buildings that were never built are buildings without shadows. Architecture drives mass through the filter of the mind. It is really the art in which the greatest opposites are combined. It has the greatest tension, and it is, of course, the most material, the most object-oriented, the most earthbound, the heaviest art in its language of form. It is materiality as none other, and yet it is pure mathematics. It mixes mystical fantasy with naked cipher. It almost always evokes the impression of power, and it tires quickly, as does everything monumental. It is sensual and yet does not touch the sentimental emotions. In a single instant its language, mostly compressed into a formula of form and function, is assimilated and understood, and still it is abiding and always present. It does not have the necessity of reproducing itself as does music through tones or literature through words. And, because it is aesthetic and functional at the same time, it is also very moral. Moral because it is public. Architecture is the most public of the arts. In every other art there are works imaginable that live only for their creator and only in the moment of their creation and that their creator can destroy immediately after their creation. In architecture the creator cannot work secretly, he must appear in public and with that appearance in public must assume responsibility in regard to the general public. Architecture is characterized by what is moral even in the form of statics. The wall must not fall, the vault not collapse. That moment of correctness and dependability brings the art that resides in cold stone and steel into the warmth of human proximity more than does any other art. And in another way we perceive architecture as human: It has it as hard in the world as does humankind itself.

In no art is the disproportion between what is theoretically conceivable and practically possible so great as here. And since this tension between wishing and capability exists generally in human life, architecture is a sublime symbol for the tension between what you want to do in your mind and what you are able to do in reality. Architecture is truly majestic—but how many sober and common requirements does it depend on! There it stands, a tower in the ages, a long shadow across the centuries—but it is relinquished to the mighty and it is dependent on their wealth. Just take the empress Maria Theresa as an example. She paid the bills for her palace in Schönbrunn, but then she burnt it so she wouldn't have the sum before her eyes.

When I brought out my series *Vedute di Roma antica e moderna,* which also contained some works by my French friends Duflos, Le Geay, and Bellichard, Bouchard again took over its distribution. It was a matter of nothing more than works for special occasions, which were distinguished by the rare combination of scientifically exact reproduction on the one hand and emotional metaphorical language on the other. Works for special occasions: For actually I always wanted only to build, to build, nothing but to build. Now as before I considered myself exclusively an architect, but not as a penny-pinching mercenary creature and illustrator of travel guides.

Many of my friends advised me, once and for all, to change over to painting, but I didn't take their recommendation seriously and cast such advice to the winds. How I detested the stupid injunction to draw the buildings exactly so that any peasant or barbarian traveling to Rome could recognize them easily. Constantly I was forced to conform to the traditional rules of *prospettiva* in order to show the traveler as many details of a building and of its ambience as possible. Because of the huge demand I was even forced to work up a stockpile. Views of interesting sights: what an insult!

I could no longer endure that and began with the poeticization of views on the side: the monument still stood in the center—but more and more I let the landscape grow into the architecture instead of merely framing it. Little by little I pushed the structures to the edge and took up a surprising or provocative attitude toward the object depicted. With such work I earned so much, at least temporarily, that I could afford my own print shop.

Of course, I did succeed in gaining a name as an engraver, but unfortunately not as an architect. My needle engraved in the service of the cult of antiquity but nevertheless dared shortened perspective and the grotesque lowering of the horizon: meager joys of a messed-up life mercilessly gone wrong. Day and night this pitiless knowledge choked me.

To escape my misery I was even forced to dedicate my work to influential figures such as Giovanni Gaetano Bottari, the confidant of three popes.

How I hated that toadying! How ashamed I was to humble myself like that. I was revolted, mostly at myself. And that constant bowing and devoted polishing of doorknobs. Yes, sir, Excellency, splendid, Excellency, just as you wish, your Excellency. Your Excellency has an extraordinary sense for art.

Enough to make you throw up!

But it was all in vain anyway: No one wanted to erect the buildings I planned, and I no longer wanted to draw them.

In order to liberate myself a bit emotionally, yes, I admit it, in order to vent my anger, I angled the depicted monuments from the upper edge of the picture, compressed the height of the image and exaggerated its dimensions, clipped the silhouettes of the columns and arches in the backlighting or let the foreground and the horizon scrunch together. My lines and the cross-hatching became fidgety, great portions of shadow got out of hand, and chunks of wall in the outlines of antique ruins and façades etched in the sparkling midday sky between bushes shifted into an imaginary distance. With its *magnificènza* Rome became more and more a ghost city for me. My concessions became fewer and fewer, the comfortable genre scenes were dominated more and more by the grotesque and comical. Light and shadow became the expression of my own emotions. With spiteful meticulousness I transformed the streets of Rome into the masked Venice of Canaletto and in so doing chose an unconventional large folio format that couldn't be more uncomfortable for travelers. Rome's monument districts demanded a monumental format. I proceeded ever more radically, unrolled the city once from a bird's-eye view and then again from the idyllic perspective of a blade of grass. However, I remained the designing architect with every line, conscientiously analyzed building after building, emphasized the construction joints, and examined the surroundings to the very edge of the city.

There was no lack of grumblers, know-it-alls, and critics. Some talked about the rhetoric of excessiveness, others about the misuse of the view as a poem of experience. And why? Only because I also included the living present. The everyday bustle around squares and fountains, the mucky streets, the unsightly dwellings, the booths and stands of the fairs, the platforms of criers and quacks, the dealers and handicraftsmen, fishwives and stallboys, beggars and scabbed persons, refined gentlemen gone astray, the tumult of wagons at the entrance to the Corso, the arrival of travelers at the Dogana, the weekly market in front of the Pantheon, the drilling militiamen, the afternoon rendezvous at the Spanish Steps, during which the nobleman was accustomed to having a chocolate in his coach, the barkers on the Piazza Navona, the strung-up wash, the shoeing of nags, dogs copulating in the middle of the street, the lustful motion of the hands of gentlemen under the skirts of the young Roman girls who presumably were seeking spiritual comfort in the nave of S. Paolo fuori le Mura, the hypocritical loathing of those lecherous mares who were only waiting to be mounted behind the altar or in the confessional.

And what was the result of all my effort? Less and less did they want to believe that I was an architect. When I set to work to expend all my energy and all my savings on a plan, I gained only a shaking of heads and boundless misunderstanding.

Ad usum architectorum I determined stubbornly to research and survey the Roman antiquities anew in order to let the Rome of antiquity again rise from the ruins and the exposed foundations. The result was a four-volume monumental work with more than two hundred and fifty etchings: *Le Antichità Romane.*

I presented exact city plans, outstanding etchings, ground plan reconstructions; I showed burial chambers, bridges, arches of triumph. Often I stripped the monuments of their modern additions and extensions and turned them into bare ruins. No contemporary could see them in that way. Only I, because I combined profound technical and archaeological knowledge with a talent for invention and imagination. The fora and the open squares have the dizzying transmutation into deep perspectives of the Baroque stage; the remains of columns in the grass also still have a defiant power as toppled fragments. I dissected masonry just as an anatomist dissects a corpse. It may be that the Enlightenment was for me nothing more than the transfiguration of antiquity. But the image is not reality, rather it only creates reality—as in every art. We know nothing about reality except that it changes.

With my companions from the French Academy I set out day after day and studied the overgrown layout of the burial structures on the Via Appia and the villas at Tivoli. Together with these few friends, even then remaining, after our extensive excursions I drafted my cyclopean structures that suddenly—I do not know why—made me of interest to the fashion-setting, better society.

I became the vogue. All the while, I knew that in artistic things *avant-garde* means little more than an agreement with some kind of philistine trend. And I hated nothing as much as the society that was involved: There you either become wounded or defiled. How quickly those who are no longer desired are gotten rid of there. And to survive fashion, isolation is the only savior. I was and am a regular refugee from events and an enemy of social gatherings. I'd rather creep away behind my closed eyelids into some corner or other, encircled by night and pretending to be asleep, wrapped in black tissue paper. In so-called social circles there is only babbling and debate about art. Nothing is so disgusting as debating and babbling about art. Everyone in the world babbled and babbles even today about art; each one felt and feels competent, and there came out and still comes out only detestable and despicable nonsense. Ladies suddenly found me handsome and fiery. But to be in fashion means allying oneself with one's own pallbearers. That's the greatest danger for an artist, because he falls victim all too readily to his own vanity. Suddenly he is surrounded by only a horde of bootlickers and hypocrites. There are artists who work in the direction their lives take and such, as I, who always travel with their backs toward their destinations.

Even critics, those pathetic dowsers with their own empty blockheads, whose misery comes from their lack of insight, begin to flatter you with a mincing face. That is especially suspicious. As soon as an artist becomes friends with a critic or falls for his hypocrisy, he is hopelessly lost. Because the knives for the next slaughter are already honed, and no critic will hesitate to make capital for his own miserable trade from familiarities so won. Critics are like the apprentices of medicine, for they always think the artist is suffering from that very ailment that they are just in the process of researching. They never write about what the artist wants and does but only about what they the critics want and then *by definition* don't find. The ridiculous critics always work with concepts, but the artist works with forms. Concepts vanish, but forms endure.

But I sensed that danger at once, made myself correspondingly scarce, unfriendly, reacted brusquely, and avoided those dreary invitations, their false and empty chatter and ignorance, for I knew that whenever it came to their support of my construction plans, the gentlemen quickly withdrew. At receptions they treated me like a rare animal. Still, behind my back, the toadies called me conceited and arrogant because I didn't follow their sneaky trails. I could trust only a very few people. In their company I felt myself somewhat protected, and we often told one another curious stories until far into the early morning hours.

I remember one story from that time because later it was to become of great importance for me. A friend and patron of the arts and at the same time a despiser of critics, the marchese di Marchi, a great gourmet, told it on the occasion of a banquet that was given in my honor in a small circle. Marchi liked best of all to tell anecdotes about cooks. It concerned several large, paté-stuffed birds—Tacchino all'Arcangeli—named for the cook who had invented this delicacy. Marchi got to know him when fifteen-year-old Arcangeli, while scuffling with several youths, suddenly threatened to use a knife on them. Marchi was pleased with the boy's fervor and took him, the son of a bankrupt and wanderer, under his wing, had him educated, and sent him to Rome, where already at the age of seventeen he became the envied cook of Count Bardi. But one day the count dismissed him because of his sudden rages, for as soon as something went against Arcangeli's wishes, he began to throw kitchen knives around. Later, Arcangeli is said to have been in Venice, Laibach, Graz, Vienna, and Pressburg with varying success. Years later the marchese di Marchi happened upon the cook again at a trial: Arcangeli had relieved his last employer of a few hundred ducats and then threatened him with a knife. Marchi had again decided to take Arcangeli, who had matured into a handsome man, into his service. And Arcangeli had expressed his gratitude with his Tacchino all'Arcangeli. This story remained in my thoughts for a long time. I did not know then how it was one day to have a connection with my own life.

Since I had to support myself for more than five years only from the sale of my older works, money became scarce. This eternal ridiculous dependency on money! And I was working as though possessed, as though I were crazy about forcing my affairs onto the whole world. I always carried pen and paper with me, and when I was forced to stop with someone for a moment, I at once sketched some kind of composition on the corner of a table. Mostly, except for a few hasty lines, there was little to see on the paper, for the work was done mainly with my mind and in my mind. I drew an enormous number of layouts, sectional views, finished detail studies, wrote broadly laid-out commentaries larded with footnotes that were spread over the sheets like fly droppings and drove the reader into a stuttering reading because they pelted down on him like hail, held fast to my observations, incorporated the state of the sciences, lost myself in boundless irrelevancies of marginal controversies.

In this time of complete overwork and total exhaustion the wind of disaster brought me a further stroke of fate that burdens me to this very day like a boulder on my soul.

Just imagine what happened to me. The most appalling thing you can think of, Heaven's trickery: Love!

I know of no happiness that would have been farther away than love. *Love is in the one who loves, not in the one who is loved*, reads Plato's maxim. Ha! Love is something like infinity but tossed to the dogs.

Back then, reason definitely left my head, for I wanted to understand not only a woman but love itself. Love, so I believed, was the stormy happiness of being alive. It was the source of that turmoil that suffers no other name than hope. But unfortunately, what's in old books about it is correct: Love snatches your heart out of your body and lays it in the snow like a bludgeoned fish. Nevertheless, I believed in love and considered it still more mighty than a holy name. Love that is engraved in your heart, I thought, could never be extinguished. What a dire mistake!

But strictly speaking, my whole existence is a mistake. I myself consider myself a dire abnormity of human nature. I am ruled by a kind of gravitation toward misfortune, a devouring annoyance that cannot be joked away, preached away, or cursed away. But hardly had I accepted that than love came along and pulled the rug out from under my feet. Whom could I have so insulted that

I was punished in this incomprehensible manner.

A man loves a woman and with that turns out the light. He then no longer lives as he did before, rather he begins to die a thousand deaths and just gropes around crazily in the darkness to dream of unrealizable things.

I was in my thirtieth year of life, and it was a stirring time. *The Coffee House* was premiered by Goldoni, Cuvilliés built the Munich Residenztheater, Egid Quirin Assam and Johann Sebastian Bach died, Johann Tobias Mayer drew the first survey map of the moon, the minuet was being danced everywhere, in London the first insane asylum was opened and the literary circle of women there wore ridiculous blue stockings, Chaumette developed the breech-loading rifle. Ladies' fashion preferred crinoline, laced-up corsets, high-heeled shoes, fans, flounces, and beauty spots, while jackets, vests, three-cornered hats, lace collars, velvet knee pants, buckled shoes, cane, and dagger were prescribed for gentlemen.

And what was I doing?

On one of those silken evenings on which the sirocco flutters its sticky batwings in your face and you are more afraid of being old and being alone than you are of death, I was falling for Angelica Pasquini, the provocatively laughing, maddeningly beautiful, what am I saying, extremely sensual daughter of a gardener of Prince Corsini, who was ensnaring me mysteriously and enigmatically: a flirt. She made me rave constantly with jealousy. Every time I looked at her, I felt my body grow heavier. And her cooing laughter dug gray lines in my face. Who does not sit in fright before the curtain of his heart? asks the poet. The misfortune of the saints is their sex. And I longed always for a lovely silly girl, demure, compliant, devoted, for one who knits her brows when she tries to understand something. The slightest probability is happiness. I believed I had conquered a palace, and yet had only scraped my knee on a wretched wall.

I offered Angelica a love that she could not comprehend at all. Anyone who has looked closely at my etchings and landscapes recognizes my conviction that the world, the transitory world, rests on a few very simple thoughts, thoughts of such simplicity that they must be as old as mountains. It rests among other things essentially on the thought of fidelity.

At the first sight of Angelica Pasquini, when I, a quaking faint-hearted soul, decided on the spot to marry that woman, my reason came to a stop, for marriage means cutting its rights in half and doubling its duties, as my grandfather had taught me. But I was blind and deaf in my devotion. With tender cynicism Angelica called me her *dear friend and copperplate engraver.* She never used my name when she addressed me, but always that phrase, which I took to from the start. In Angelica's arms I mimicked Don Juan and let my wishes dance on her tongue. Becoming familiar with the body of a woman resembles a circumnavigation of the world without a compass. But she wore her nakedness with the elegance of a cat. With pride in having invented a new kind of caress, I showed her my etchings. But she only laughed. Later her sighs meant: this eternal building stuff. I was surprised by her experience in things of love. That should have disconcerted me. She was a woman about whom poems are made. A glance from her cat's eyes were enough to turn any man into a lackey on the spot. Her gaze blinded mirrors. When I married Angelica, my friends said nothing, left their sinister prophecies unsaid. But Angelica wouldn't stop babbling; I could have cut out her tongue.

Anyone who acts out of love leaves himself wide open.

I remember well the day I fell in love with Angelica. It was in the hottest month of the year. The city lay muggy under the vibrating air. In the inner courtyards birds sat dizzily in the bushes, ornamental fish floated belly up in the ponds, leaves shriveled as though it had become autumn, crickets chirped as though they were being roasted alive.

At the time I did not yet suspect that any woman who pretends to love has a scorpion in her lap.

Angelica! She bent under my first kisses like a sapling, and the aroma of freshly peeled apples lay on her skin.

If you could summon death with mere thoughts the way you can love, then many would lay stretched out every night. But in reality a person in that condition doesn't have a clear thought.

Oh, she was as beautiful as a full moon. The colors of life beamed in her face. Her skin was as smooth as soapstone, her legs like polished copper, her unruly hair blue-black as the wing of a crow.

Angelica: that green net, when she narrowed her eyes. After a few nights when her body glowed next to me, we glided apart like ships and an infinitely long time of the most horrible torture began. She made me more forsaken than a slain man in a gutter.

Angelica: Your vows were false, your promises were empty and deeply hypocritical.

Angelica: My love for you was the deepest and darkest dungeon into which I threw myself.

Angelica: In her veins the blood had trickled away to ice. And while she breathed into my face, she could rub her breasts against a man who was standing yards away.

My jealousy, controlled during the daytime by work, broke out all the more strongly at night into dreams that often enough ended with loud sobs. Only much later was I to find out that the years with Angelica were more beautiful in memory than they were in reality. Original sin came from a woman, and we all must die because of her, but in my delusion I believed you can walk through life only hand in hand. As for Angelica, I never knew whether it was love or hysteria. Did I at all know what I wanted from that woman at all?

You can never know what you ought to want because you have only one life, which you cannot compare with an earlier life or correct in a later one.

Soon after our hasty marriage Angelica presented me with the puzzle of her presumably delicate health. Little by little it became the basis for a prerogative that lasted all our lives, of never being completely there—the right to withdraw, that is, to climb into the bed of one of her numerous lovers and to cuckold me not in a small way but in an enormous way.

A marriage consists of the circumstance of two people being telescoped into what is unendurable, like geological seams of stone. Constantly living with a woman is a form of existence that cannot be more unnatural. It was to me as though I had married a monster. On the other hand, she presumably had the impression that she had bound herself to a ghost who was as maniacally jealous as he was a workaholic.

Angelica *animale:* Hardly an afternoon passed without her having visitors or making visits. No one turned down an invitation to her evening socials, at which she displayed her sensuous body in the most daring and expensive clothes. She loved robes of heavy, glittering cloth with enticing bodices.

Angelica: *passiflora mia!* Her dark-red lips, always with lipstick on them, with their slightly smug curve, hardly moved when she spoke. Her sharply tapered hands had a magic authority about them. They arranged things exactly the way this woman wanted them to be. There was a power in her glances that struck every man acutely.

Angelica had all the gifts of a *cortigiana*, a pretty-sounding word that makes you think of courtly ladies and yet means *whore*. She esteemed all the delights of the life of a courtesan, such as summertime stays in the country in princely gardens, musical gondola rides, and flirtatious drives and nights of love, no matter whether with beardless youths, rich bachelors, listless husbands, generous, more mature gentlemen, randy songsters. They just had to have something, for if they had nothing, then they got nothing either. Whenever Angelica swore to me, if she happened at the moment to be in the mood, how mortally in love she was only with me, I didn't believe a word she said. *It is impossible that a woman, before whom the whole world lies prostrate, feels love for any man at all.* Aretino wrote that in his *Dialogues*. Angelica had the burning ambition to prepare for her lovers not only physical but also spiritual pleasures. Of course, she was musical, had an enchanting voice, and played the lute marvelously. But she understood nothing about art.

As far as art is concerned, the female sex has always done only damage, for women lack any sense for what is artistic. At best they have a certain intelligence of Eros, which of course is different from that of the mind. Women's only accomplishment consists of taking from thought what is serious about it: clarity, depth, anxiety. You can best recognize a clever woman in her keeping the work of female and male authors strictly separate in her library. But a woman is always considered the most magnificent and adored creature. Every artist always fell to his knees before women. Only women have experienced that glorification over the centuries, but never men. Mothers are idolized anyway only because with terrifying moans they squeeze these poor little creatures out of themselves again and again. And if today everything is traced back to mothers, then they must certainly also be the cause for the supposed suppression of women. In addition, women always held the power because they are more cunning by nature. Today, nothing in the world is more sheltered than a woman. And nothing gobbles up money more foolishly. Just think of the huge sums swallowed up by preparations for a daughter's wedding. Daughters want nothing more than to be married constantly. The incessant talk about the suppression of women is again just women's malice. While men fully display intellect and emotion, women have only emotion. And they use it mostly against men. The so-called intellect of women is nothing more than an emotion dolled up as intellect. A pack of lies. Pure intellectual hypocrisy. As soon as women are exposed to intellectual resistance, they capitulate and bring their bodies or emotions into play because they have no other resources that they can make use of. For that reason women are untiringly occupied with their bodies. They oil and anoint and lubricate them, constantly take one or another ludicrous bath or run to the doctor. Even the sight of a woman's figure teaches you that the female is not meant either for great intellectual or physical labors, says the philosopher. Women cling unswervingly to the present, take appearances for the real thing, prefer trifles and all kinds of trumpery to important matters, are by nature supplied with the gift of playacting like a steer with horns, have no sense for art but only for domineering, bickering, a desire to please, and babbling that they are not able to put aside even at the sight of a Michelangelo. Men see all of that but remain silent because they are dazzled. If I can rouse a certain sympathy for the Greeks, then it's only because they kept their women out of the theater. To call this sex the beautiful can have occurred only to a man befogged by his sex drive.

I remember a meeting with a namesake, the violin virtuoso Viotti. His father was a village blacksmith in Fontanetto Po, a small town in the province of Vercelli, halfway between Turin and Novara. In my time Viotti was the world's best violinist. No one played as he did, and I doubt that anyone ever attained his importance. His playing put everything else in the shade. I liked Viotti. He was an unhappy wretch. In spite of his thunderous success in Paris, Dresden, Berlin, Warsaw, St. Petersburg, and London, he put down his bow at the age of twenty-eight from one day to the next, never to appear in public again. Paris lay at his feet, but although he was assailed from all sides, he did not offer any reasons for his decision. I heard Viotti: his violin Concerto no. 23 in C Minor. The andante. Four minutes and forty-five seconds. There is no better definition of pain and music. Immediately afterward I had the good fortune to chat a while with Viotti. We became close at once; we recognized one another at first sight. What did we talk about? About art? The godlike Viotti said only: My father was a blacksmith. He shoed horses to a beat. My music comes from him. Then, of course, we talked about women. Viotti, who as a manager also let his orchestra play without a director, gave me a peek into his private hell: Women suffer less from a separation, above all when they themselves leave. They come to terms easier with it because their emotions are only superficial. Marriage? With what eyes do you look at a farce that you have fought for mutually? Most women lust after successful men. They admire nothing more than they do success. If their social status bestows no sense of achievement upon them, then at least their husbands must be successful. Woman as the first critic and the first admirer of the artist, woman as the refuge in crises and awful hours! If I hear that again! If among a hundred women you find an exception, then she has tits as stingy as a goat's, or she's cross-eyed. Or she stinks of garlic. And as far as offering refuge is concerned, I'm afraid it's like admiration: It doesn't last long. Dirty underwear, farts in bed, breath that smells of wine, nose picking, tiredness, because you have written music or etched copperplate until late at night and are exhausted: That's how the artist looks in everyday life. He has flaws like any other human being. He has even more of them than others do, and the woman who chooses to admire him, soon sees only the flaws. She simply pretends admiration when guests are present. Then she pats her husband and calls him a big kid patronizingly. And as soon as the guests are gone, she points to the spots on his jacket and says: You're a big pig! She understands nothing of the misery of composition or etching copper, of all the agony: nothing. Whenever he complains, she thinks of it as sniveling or pathological fuss. He's oversensitive, she says to her girl friends and lovers; with every little complaint he screams bloody murder—that's how she thinks she has to apologize for him, and she's never caught on that that's just what makes him an artist. Perhaps you will accuse me of generalizing too much. Let's say that you find the understanding woman, the ideal artist's wife, who protects you from the daily grind, listens to you patiently, supports you. How long do you think she can keep doing that? Certainly not for all her life, not living with you. A bad mood is her normal state. My friend Cherubini has a wife— she exudes her bad mood regularly; the whole house is full of bad mood; hardly is the door opened and you sense it. The bad mood hits you with a stink. Have you ever seen men who can constantly be in a bad mood the way women can? A woman takes it upon herself all day long to wear grumpily in her face whatever doesn't suit her. Or that nothing at all suits her. There is no use asking: What doesn't suit you today, madam? You're what doesn't suit her. You alone! Where a man swallows or makes a gesture of dismissal for the sake of peace or because trifles are simply not worth taking seriously, a woman puts on a sour face and makes an affair of state out of nothing. Whenever men quarrel, it's about the matter at hand. As soon as everything is cleared up, the quarrel is also over. Women are never concerned about the matter at hand but about persons and about their benefit. It always concerns *bella figura*. Females never quarrel because they have an opinion different from someone but because they don't like that someone. When women quarrel among themselves, they always start pulling hair first. They quarrel for quarrel's sake. So men are by nature conciliatory, but women are by nature quarrelsome. Cicadas are blessed because their females are mute.

I liked that crazy Viotti. He was a man after my own taste. Later he founded a theater with the hairdresser of Marie-Antoinette, but then went to London and became a wine dealer. Until the impoverished end of his life he suffered from an unfulfilled love.

To conclude from the number of servants and the luxury of the furnishings of her house, you could have believed that Angelica was a princess. Salon, bedchamber, and boudoir were so splendidly furnished that you saw nothing but velvet and brocades and expensive carpets on exquisite tiles. The walls were draped with golden fabrics, the curtains hung richly embroidered and pleated, the mantelpieces were decorated with ultramarine as well as arrayed with vases of alabaster, porphyry, and serpentine. Everywhere richly filled chests and small tables ornamented with costly intarsia stood in rows.

And who paid for all that junk, who worked for it day and night to total exhaustion for the pittance of a smile? I paid for it with my ridiculous and pathetic life gone wrong, even though Angelica also contributed some from her whore's wages, because she demanded a considerable honorarium for her favors. She was as shrewd as she was good at business. Soon she was earning more with her screwing around than I ever did with my art, which brought me additional scornful snide remarks from her: You and your eternal building nonsense! Her extravagant hairstyles, which required hours-long preparation, her expensive gowns of black silk and golden pendants, the rings and pearls and chains as well as her veiled and unveiled physical charms Angelica preferred to show off during the mass in S. Maria della Pace and S. Agostino, the traditional churches for whores in Rome. Angelica, from the beginning accustomed to having her body admired, was an eager churchgoer, for she enjoyed it when men stood in line languishing at the portals. She knew exactly how to put silly ideas into men's heads, how to create friends and lure money from their purses. Angelica sold her body more often than ordinary streetwalkers the innocence of their daughters. For those kinds of pleasures they all had money: bankers, prelates, bishops, cardinals, diplomats, but not where I and my plans were concerned. Cleverly, Angelica switched with her demanding vanity between denial and affection and always paid attention to the wealth, rank, and influence of her admirers, in order to bask in it. But she didn't raise a finger, of course, for me and my interests. Among her admirers Angelica had the honorary appellation *La Tortora,* that is, the turtle dove, but for me this woman, do pardon this poor joke, was only *La Tortura.*

Angelica: She practically dared you to lay a hand on her. She presented herself as a trophy and yet was still the huntress with eyebrows like arching crossbeams and with her proud nose that gave her face that arrogance that everyone fell for. Whoever she ignored felt branded, but whoever she then finally had in bed after the customary fooling around, to which she attached great importance, he noticed fairly quickly what a pitiful occasion it was. But her body was always warm and restless, hungry and unendurably lascivious. In bed she was like a cat that sleeps indolently on the sheet. Whenever she was fucked, birds seemed to fly out of her mouth, and her body twitched like a bludgeoned fish. But the man always found himself in a kind of unsuccessful state of besiegement. I never slept with another woman after Angelica but practiced asceticism that did not come from abstention but from the impossibility in the future of taking other, lesser pleasures.

Angelica: She had insatiable thighs and wild, bushy hair in her armpits, real nests; her nipples were large and pink, and when I licked them, they turned saddle brown, almost black.

How curious to fall in love with a body and its enticements, which reeks and inexorably goes to ruin. How can you fall for a woman because of whom a few years later you would change sides of the street so as not to meet her?

Three children crept out of her womb, but only one was squeezed from my loins, as I was to find out only years later. They were ugly and terrible children, who wheedled neither stories nor sweets from me. Three years into the marriage the girl Laura was born. Petrarch and my mother sent their greetings. Three years later came my son Francesco. Finally, Pietro followed. I don't even want to know who his father was. Only monsters erupt from between such thighs.

One should give up the illusion of duplicating oneself. Those children were my gravediggers.

Hardly marriageable, Laura sold a series of miniature copies of my etchings cheap; spoiled Pietro ended up completely dissolute, while Francesco at least understood how to make the best deals with my work. Admittedly, he helped with the plates of the views of Paestum, also occasionally stood in the way in the studio and pulled off a few editions and supplementary volumes. Finally he brought out a complete catalogue of his published products, for which he thought up thirty-two subdivisions. He was even appointed by the Swedish king Gustav III, who was staying in Rome, to be the royal agent for the fine arts in Italy. In return he soon sold the largest part of my museum in the Palazzo Tomati to Stockholm, was appointed the Swedish consul in Naples, and operated as a counterspy. After a four-year stay in Naples he returned to Rome and, with his half brother Pietro, became a Jacobin in order to serve the short-lived Tibernian Republic, which was propped up by French bayonets. After its collapse because of English and Napoleonic troops, only flight to Paris remained, where Francesco wanted to build a new life on my plates. In addition, he produced miserable terra-cotta copies of the antiquities of my museum. And he himself tried the cold needle with moderate talent and meager success. He did not even come close to my mastery. A talent must want no boundaries, not only loyalty. Had Columbus been loyal to the egg, he would never have discovered the New World. With Francesco's death the family enterprise also collapsed. Since then my etchings have been scattered all over the world. Many hang in galleries and museums.

That's naturally absurd, revolting, and repulsive, for pictures are not suited to hang one after the other on a bare wall in front of which nothing more than pushing and shoving takes place. The most unprincipled dealers are still doing business with them. And still I have thrown away more etchings and landscapes and sketches and plans and sheets than I published.

We always wish to have children different from those that we get finally just so they can shovel out our graves while we are alive. Making a child always means making bad luck.

What time, energy, and money did that selfish and vain cocotte Angelica cost me! I suffered most from her fickleness. I could not depend on any of her words, on any of her pledges. It didn't even take half an hour for her to do the opposite of what she had promised me before. I ran along behind her like a dog, whined, howled, raved, scratched on her door, but she never let me in. Now she said this, then again that. Nothing was certain. I couldn't plan on anything. And if I ever raised quiet criticism, then she was at once mortally offended and forced me to crawl anew. I even forgot myself to such an extent that I asked pardon for the injustice and the humiliations that she committed against me. Not even a good hiding would have improved Angelica. But please don't misunderstand me: Of course, I never even touched a hair of her head. On the contrary, I worshiped her. The energy simply to throw her out, which my closest friends steadily advised me to do because they could no longer look on at how I suffered and languished more and more—I didn't have that energy. I loved that woman. For a time she even forbade me to see her, although we were married. She took trips and indiscriminately met her numerous lovers, who prowled around one another like tomcats and with whom she pulled me and my idolatrous love into the dirt in public in the worst way. I confronted her again and again, but every time her reply sounded like the cooing of doves. Whenever she came back home again, I gave her presents that she didn't

even open but lay aside unnoticed. And she was constantly
stricken by a mania for finery as though by an incurable illness.
Being in fashion means nothing more than to give up one's individuality. Angelica's jewelry boxes sat all over the place: velvet
coffins of my preposterous love. My attempt to let Angelica live
for eternity in words is as silly as it is puny, for my words may well
encompass worlds and seas but never her essence.

At that time I presumably worked so self-destructively only to
try to impress that woman, who thought nothing at all of my
etchings. There appears to be passion only for what is opposite.

Of course, in my jealousy my behavior was totally preposterous.
Too often I banged my skull against the corner of a table and just
wanted to bleed all over everything. Jealousy throttles any good
sense. I knew I was ridiculous and pathetic, and yet I believe that
a jealous person deserves not our scorn but, in his pain, much
more our honest sympathy. I tell you: These are horrible torments
that are suffered by those who are jealous. Horrible. They think
their intestines are being pulled through their gullets. More and
more the air they breathe is taken away. They think they are
smothering, and the more imagination they have, the more dread-
fully they suffer. Can you imagine what that meant for a man with
my fantasy? Can you possibly imagine that? Only so-called
human beings without any kind of fantasy are unacquainted with
jealousy. But with malicious glee all the more. It's the worst trait
in human nature. Mostly malicious glee steps in where sympathy
should have its place. And I was in urgent need of a point of rest
in my life. What I longed for was a true and good soul who would
place a warm blanket across my withered knees in my old age. But
Angelica, that egotistical creature, drove me again and again to
the edge of collapse and beyond.

Altogether a highly tragic situation on which I don't want to waste a further word except to state that with wise foresight I invested Angelica's dowry in expensive copperplates for my etchings.

Now and again one of Angelica's lovers turned up, made a frightful scene, shredded my expensive sheets, or scratched up my costly copperplates. Irascible brawls broke out, in which, because of my rather frail physical constitution, I got the short stick. If you don't have muscles, you are lost. Only with effort and with the assistance of a few apprentices did I succeed from time to time in throwing those guys out of my workshop. But Angelica seemed only amused by that. She made a snippy face or sulked until I came crawling up again and begged her forgiveness for what she had done to me.

And yet, you don't love because of but in spite of.

I numbed myself with work, work, work.

I knew that I *had* to build!

Pierced by this revelation of *having* to build, which drummed down upon me with the excessive persistence of a waterfall, I faded away at the same time.

Archaeological observation, meticulous measuring, and fantastic reconstruction—as I tried to persuade myself, what am I saying, tried to hammer into myself—were more important than the flirting of a spoiled female with the body of a goddess, the disposition of a butcher, and the brain of a sparrow. It cost me years of my life to liberate myself to some extent from Angelica, but I never ever overcame that pain completely. Now as before she appears in my worst dreams, and she always lies in the arms of a different man and does it with him. Today I know all that this woman killed off in me in the shabbiest and basest way.

On top of that came the misery of not being permitted to build. That and Angelica made me completely and eternally into a ludicrous figure. Ludicrous! Do you understand? Or is there anything more ludicrous than a *becco*, a cuckold who imagines that he is a great architect and yet always, scratching around on copperplate with the cold needle, is allowed to pursue only the eccentric figments of his imagination?

The architect today can design any city, even on the moon. But he can't build it—a repetition of my life gone wrong. That's why one architect's vision is as good today as any other's. All that remains these days is pretend architecture, mirror architecture: the reflection of an infinite, detached power of imagination. Beyond that are the real cities: just as abysmally ugly as they are inhuman. Only the *favelas* of Rio de Janeiro or on Smoky Mountain in Manila are still built imaginatively. Some architects today want to bring the so-called environment into harmony with so-called humankind freely and cleverly, while others proclaim that proportions are what is infinite. But secretly all architects today declare themselves to be the Titans of the earth and rivals of the Creator, whom they murder with every stroke on their sketch paper. They long for a great overseer, and each of them believes secretly that he is a man of initiative. They believe themselves to be a Messianic creator, through whom humankind can rise to God. Nature is so arranged, they believe, that so-called humankind, wherever it is, must feel it is the center of the universe. Their message is the novelty of the new: with ancient means. The so-called new cities reflect this world in a treacherous way: as the appropriation of Nature by humankind. Heartiest congratulations! Childish as they are, the architects of today assume that the world has no shape beyond their own plans. They deceive themselves.

Thoroughly! Architects see themselves as self-appointed gods who contemplate the salvation of humankind. Not only are theirs the voices of superiority and self-exaggeration but also of longing and not having evidence to offer for this: because they understand architecture as world salvation and themselves as its executors. That's why they style themselves as prophets and guides to the true life in order to proclaim a new age in shining cities. But the salvation of the world through architecture never took place.

For the infinite freedom of human imagination has its boundaries—to the extent that it becomes practical. In what is practical it can also be boundless—if it is prepared to destroy. If it wants to be creative, it must attain within bounds what it aims to bring about: the figure sought in forms that it observes; the completion striven for in solutions that it has found; the desired association in structures that it has discovered. Each one who is creative shapes what he shapes in forms, solutions, structures that he doesn't know, doesn't have to know as long as he doesn't set out to produce something or shape something or build something. But if he does set out to do something, he enters the creative process, to make something definite from something indefinite, something associated from something disassociated; for example, if he enters into the creative process of an architect, to build the form of a house from the materials of the earth, in the expanse of the land to lay out the boundaries of a city. The freedom of modern city planners also has limits. Only in their proclamations did they build out of a void—like gods. In their practice, however, they stepped into the world of the circle, the square, the axis of the world, the coordinate system: They remained human beings.

I have never succeeded in changing from a ridiculous figure to a laughing figure. What makes people like me inevitably into a ridiculous person is the earnestness with which we deal with a particular present time only because it has the appearance of being important. But in the final analysis everything falls victim to ridicule or at least to pity, no matter how great or important it may be. In the end we control only what we also find ridiculous, said the architect of the wheel of history and the unfolder and extinguisher of his universal drama; only when we find the world and life on it ridiculous do we move forward; there is no other, no better method.

I knew only one thing—I *had* to build!

So please believe me. You must have me confused with someone else. I am not Piranesi. My name is Cheval, Ferdinand Cheval, born on April 19, 1836, in Charmes-sur-l'Herbasse, Départment Drôme, died on August 17, 1924, in Hauterives on the banks of the Galaure. As a rural postman I walked daily in a region where the sea left visible traces of its sojourn—once I walked in snow and ice, once in blooming fields. What was I to do? If you walk eternally in the same splendor, if not dream? I dreamed. In order to divert my thoughts, in dream I built a fairy-tale palace that exceeded my imagination and everything that the genius of a humble man may contrive, with grottoes, towers, gardens, mansions, museums, and sculptures, trying to bring all earlier architectures to life again. Three years before, I had passed over that great equinox that is called the forties. This is no longer the age of crazy enterprise and castles in the clouds. But in the moment that my dream little by little sank into the fog of the past, an incident suddenly brought it to life again: My foot struck a rock that made me almost fall down. I wanted to see my stumbling block up close; it had such a remarkable shape that I picked it up from the ground and took it home with me. The next day I returned to the same spot and found even more beautiful ones that, gathered in a heap, made a nice impression. That inspired me. I said to myself: Because Nature has delivered the sculptures, I want to become an architect and mason. Who isn't part mason? And while I continued on my way, I thought:

> *The word* impossible *exists no more,*
> *The mailman has also overcome it.*
> *With this rock, I wanted to prove,*
> *What the will is capable of.*

That's when the long journey home began; it lasted twenty-five years. By covering still dozens more kilometers in addition to my daily rounds during that period of time, I filled my pockets with stones; then I used baskets, which increased my toil even more, for every day I had a round of thirty-two kilometers to finish. In the year 1879 I began the construction of the Palais Idéal. After thirty-three years of daily labor the building was finished. A towering termite construction, glued together with secretions. Stones, seashells, roots, mosses. Covered with gray dough, kneaded, churned, everywhere the feeling of my hand that fit these chunks together, chunks seemingly drenched with spittle. I dreamed. Out of impulses, thoughts, I erected forms. Here I overcame my shadowy life, lifted it out of beginning and ending and delivered it to Nature, let it lie as a monstrous construction in the garden of the world, exposed to gradual weathering under very great spans of time. With single-minded consistency I dug, burrowed, shoveled, built with masonry on my visions, scratched, scraped, polished them in tireless devotion. I grew with my dream. I didn't calculate. My reason was turned off. I followed only the voice that grew rampant deep within me. This turmoil of names—reaching inside one another, making one another illegible, erasing one another—brought the material to completion. This work is a piece of Nature. It grew without purpose, it unfolded like a blossom, branched out, sprouted new impulses. Its beauty is instinctive and flatters no one. Others take their dream, which lasts a whole life long, into insane asylums, sink down there in the mustiness of their incarceration. But the mailman succeeded in making his dream material and, by doing so, in saving his life. In the eyes of his neighbors he is a harmless crazy guy; they've gotten used to him: He's doing some masonry work on his garden grotto. When he was a child we saw him even then shoveling, scraping, and polishing; now that he's grown we still see him shoveling, scraping, and polishing. To his neighbors, who laugh at him, he just shows his peasant industry in the shape of plates of text—he's become too shy to speak, knows only his murmured soliloquy. Heureux l'homme libre brave et travailleur. Le rêve d'un paysan. *Just as the architect demonstrates his industry in his plates, he also measures his work by external criteria—he calls our attention to the fact that the east façade is twenty-six meters long, the west façade twenty-six meters long, the north façade fourteen meters long, the south façade ten meters long, the height varying between eight and ten meters. But these measurements prove nothing. He is not an artist, he is only a dreamer, and a dreamer cannot explain his dream, caught up in it as he is. Genius is industry, he scratches into the wall. Walking around the construction, you come across motifs everywhere on which his imagination found nourishment, motifs that he incorporated into his own walls and that appear as parallel themes: the columns before the burial chambers of the pharaohs, the Babylonian gate arches, the mosques of Islam, the temples of the Hindus, the pyramids of the Incas, the palaces from* A Thousand and One Nights, *the Algerian citadels, the vases and urns of antiquity, medieval castles, antediluvian snails, exotic animals, tropical plants, heathen gods, and the groups of the prophets and evangelists and the pilgrims to the Holy Tomb and the grotto of the Grail and the labyrinths and catacombs—all preserved in the structure of his soul and reworked. This work exists silently. In seclusion. It does not display itself. It perseveres in the earth from which it grew. In the burial chamber of the palace I formed two stone coffins in Saracen style as a tombs for me and for my wife. Church and congregation denied me that right. So in 1914 I bought a concession for a grave in the cemetery of Hauterives and in eight years of work created Le Tombeau de Silence et du Repos sans fin.*

You must be confusing me with someone else. I swear I'm not Piranesi. My name is Cheval, Ferdinand Cheval, born on April 19, 1836 . . .

Repeatedly I was magically drawn to the memorials and the avenues of tombs that I wanted to preserve from inexorable deterioration. I exposed numberless burial chambers, and I saw that the remains of the ancient structures of Rome, which in large part were strewn over gardens and other spaces used for agriculture, shrunk more from day to day, in part through the devastations of time, in part through the greed of their owners, who plundered and surreptitiously tore down the ruins with barbaric equanimity in order to turn them into objects of speculation and to sell the stones at a high price for use in new construction. In regard to many of these monuments I not only reproduced their external appearances but also their ground plans and interiors; I differentiated the individual parts through cross sections and elevations and indicated the materials and occasionally also the means of construction. The work grew under my hands. I examined, measured anew, and from scattered relics reconstructed far more than thirty burial structures. In doing so, I also was able to point out archaeological successes—after all, I did find the sarcophagus of the emperor Alexander Severus and his mother, Julia Mamea, whose reliefs depicted the reconciliation of the Romans and Sabines by Romulus. Naturally, I was not content with portraying all the decorative stuccos and objects found in a sepulcher or a columbarium: vases, terra-cotta vessels for ointments and ashes, styluses, needles, and ivory hair accessories. I also recorded the inscriptions and etched gravestone after gravestone. My etchings were meant to take the place of the depicted structure completely for the observer, in every detail; they were meant to become one with it. I neither omitted the condition of the walls nor the change in brickwork, the thickness and substance of the plasterwork, the delicate or more coarse relief of the stucco. And along with that I depicted the lively activity among the ruins of gout-bent old people and shameless youths who climbed heedlessly over the scattered skeletons of the ruins. Over all of that I laid an odor of mold and decay, invigorated every individual block of marble, emphasized the symmetry of the technique of interstices, and pointed out every bungling by sloppy masons. For the sake of completeness I additionally revealed the method of lifting that had allowed the Romans to cope with weight in a superhuman way. I demonstrated my stupendous knowledge as an expert on statics and as an engineer with cable winches and lifting apparatuses and sketched adjustable metal chocks and double-bent clamps that could be spread out in the interiors of the walls.

Having in my youth sketched theater sets and shadowy flights of stairs of a gloomy world of dungeons, I now concentrated with gouge and drawing pen on blocks of walls and arch supports, on long rows of bulging ashlars and flat tiles. The age of perspectives that outdid themselves seemed past.

The picture of Hadrian's Mausoleum doubtless marks the high point of this time. On two folded, attached sheets a meter and a half long I drafted an unprecedented depiction of the layout of the foundation. With the power of my imagination I placed myself back in the time of Hadrian and with his master architects and stonemasons built the whole structure once more. When I began to measure and draw Hadrian's Villa in Tivoli from the ground up, I had to clear paths for myself with an ax through the brambles and afterward start a fire to drive away snakes and scorpions. That's why many a nincompoop thought me a sorcerer.

Finally I was able to build—if again only on the copperplate.

Every detail stood before my eyes: from the pile grating rammed deep into the ground, past the different stone arrangements of the walls and the supporting arches and abutments that served to relieve the weight, to the marble slabs on which the cylinder of the mausoleum rests. I saw every position of every individual stone, the form of the wall unit, the alternation of hewn and unhewn ashlars of travertine and peperine. I reveled in the realm of Titans with a mania for building. Finally there were those who measured up to my talent; I finally had the task that corresponded to my genius. For good reason I set the observer at the very bottom and from the upper edge of the picture let the massive stone abutments plunge down like a waterfall. No one before me had dared such complex structures, and not even the know-it-all greenhorns of the Academy could refute me in their endless debates about the reliability of my measurements, so meticulous and clean were my elevation and detail drawings, so unshakable were my statics. On not less than forty folio pages I gave explanations and offered the reader the possibility of an imaginary tour at my hand around the Aurelian city wall, through the Campus Martius, and over the Quirinal, in a wide curve past the Esquiline, the Caelian, and the Aventine to Trastevere and back to the Palatine.

But that didn't suffice for me: In cellars, too, and even under garden walls I searched for the continuation of ancient traces of brick, on Monte Celio had digging done for buried arcades, urged the lazy laborers to work harder, got annoyed around the foremen, and from baked rubble reconstructed the fillwork of vanished architectures. No source was too meager for me: Everything was evaluated, even the conceited reports about the continued use of columns and travertine ashlars, about the places where important groups of marbles, sarcophagi, and ceremonial vases were found. I shied away from no digression, however boring, to clarify the original course of a street or the cohesion of a group of structures. I triumphed, but the road to that triumph was paved with nothing but disappointments.

While the elegant society of Rome's babblers and those who shot off their mouths gossiped about me again and with lustful envy reproached me for Caesarean delusion, while the young academicians and the honorable professors discussed all night long the building techniques of the ancient Romans and the topography that I suggested, I experienced anew a deep human disappointment. It concerned my would-be patron, the young art-crazy Irish peer James Caulfeild, Lord Charlemont, to whom I was ready to dedicate my work, if he should take on the role of my patron.

Again the winds of disaster blew about me.
The matter dragged on unnecessarily and was thwarted frequently by the most imaginative intrigues of those who envied me that ran around on whispered paths behind my back until finally, exaggerated gigantically, they caught up with me. Letters did not arrive, false replies were transmitted, misunderstandings fomented; as always in our awful profession the scandalmongers pocketed more than the creators. Again and again His Lordship postponed a definitive agreement, the publication date approached, the papal imprimatur granted, orders had already arrived from all of Europe, even from Scandinavia and Russia, soon more than seventy copies were sold to wealthy antiquarians and antiquity societies. Recognition was coming from everywhere—but no longed-for commission to build. His Lordship wrapped himself in refined silence and in that way never saw the four dedication plates. If I didn't want to make a fool of myself publicly, then I had no other choice than to stop delivery. I had to maneuver in the worst way and waste time and effort with senseless pamphlets. Finally, because of the hesitation of His Lordship, which I don't understand to this day, I decided to remove all references to him in my work. I celebrated the erasure of the dedication as a *damnatio memoriae* after the example of the emperor Caracalla and banned the procrastinating lord once and for all from the world of arts and sciences by visibly tearing the bronze

letters from the inscription, knocked off half the insignia carved into marble before I attached a new eulogy to the city of Rome above them. So that the symbolic gesture would also be understood correctly and would find its spectacular way through the alleyways, I added to my *Lettere di giustificazione* the inscription changed by Caracalla on his father's Arch of Triumph and sent them to prelates, artists, and cavaliers, so my deed also made the rounds among the old gossips.

Did I say *example?* No, I never had nor wanted an example. I always wanted to be only myself:

I knew: I *had* to build.

I was now thirty-six years old: Mozart had been born, a Seven Years' War began to rage on the other side of the Alps, an observatory had been established in Vienna—and I still had not built. That thorn inexorably caused havoc in me. Of course, I had succeeded decisively in promoting interest in ancient Rome and archaeology, in directing attention to the water viaducts, to the Tivoli, Albano, and Castel Gandolfo, but I remained an unhappy creature, and none of my wealthy admirers thought of giving me a commission to build.

That hurt me deeply. What was the admiration that I received even from the Russian czarina worth? Gossip, only cheap gossip. Through my experiences I had succeeded in deciphering the Medusa face of fame. People, but artists particularly, love fame and success because this means good fortune to almost all of them and, in whatever form, a copy of what they would like to be in their heart of hearts. The glory of fame beautifies everything, life scintillates as never before. Everything that you see, that you feel, taste, smell, hear in moments of fame seems enormously exaggerated in an exciting way because fame is at your side. All turmoil and weariness, all gloomy doubt and all bitter hopelessness disappear. Fame makes even silence eloquent, and even what is unspoken resounds. That's why it is so pursued by artists. The obsession for fame sits deep in the human heart. It is one of the mightiest desires of man, and because it is so deeply hidden in him, it is most grudgingly acknowledged—least of all by those who feel its sharp thorn most intensely. The temple of fame, as the philosopher says, is inhabited mostly by the dead who during their lives were not in it and by a few living, almost all of whom, when they die, will be tossed out.

Fame was denied to me as much as prosperity was. So nothing more remained for me but to head for the source of income that had financed me in recent years and the labor on my monumental work, which now was ebbing: the *Vedute di Roma*.

The series needed urgently to be added to, especially since Giuseppe Vasi, my former teacher, as a competitor had gotten out of reach on the market. Within the shortest time I had to produce a series of places of interest, fountains, squares, and churches, to get money. Again I had to set aside my building plans. The insatiable Angelica could not get enough of her luxurious life. Her wishes were inexhaustible, her craving unquenchable. Her mania for extravagance forced me to send letters with the following sad content to diverse expensive shops:

I will not accept a financial obligation for any debts or bills or promissory notes that are signed by Angelica Pasquini.

She should, after all, be kept by her lovers! Gossip-ridden Roman society again had something on which they could whet their beaks.

With inexorable industry I set to work and gave free rein to my despondency insofar as I surrendered to my propensity for the bizarre and macabre. As a gesture of defiance to the humiliation of time and society, which stubbornly denied me the chance to build, I worked with profound contrasts of light and browned shadows, increased dramatic effect by melancholic transfiguration, omitted no scratch and no irregular notch. Every damaged ornament was a mirror of my own state of mind, every gap in a wall a cut into my soul. As though in defiance I hung the dirty underclothes of whores in front of once dignified temples and placed drawbars and wheels of cartwrights against holy walls. As attributes of destructive and declining times and in order to reveal the imbalance between the heedless present and the heroic past, I populated the streets with beggars and shady characters. So I held up to society the mirror of this city, which tottered between grandeur and hopelessness, and chose the head of Janus as the symbol of my view of the world: I had to waste my time on that kind of work for a living, whereas I was, after all, an architect.

Of course, in the meantime I was chosen as a corresponding member of the London Society of Antiquaries and through fortunate circumstances had risen—or should I better say fallen—to a confidant of the pope and his favored relatives, but this did not brighten my mood, rather darkened it even more. Only a commission to build equal to my genius could have saved me. Perhaps, I hoped, a move helped; perhaps adversity clung to my house; perhaps it stood at an intersection of disastrous arteries. At first I moved from the Corso to the Spanish quarter and set up my printing operation in the Palazzo Tomati, not least of all simply to escape the constant, nerve-shredding domestic bickering.

From my new address on Strada Felice I hoped for some good fortune. Most of the furniture seemed superfluous to me; I simply gave it away or left it standing in the street. My new dwelling was supposed to be furnished in a Spartan way and provided only with the most necessary things. As difficult as I found it to sleep, I decided from now on to spend the night in my workshop, which had become my lead chamber, where it smelled of printer's ink, fish, and dirty socks. A simple cot, a couple of blankets, a table, and my books, the beloved books: I didn't want to allow myself more. I respected this scattered light in the damp, hot hell of my dungeon, in which I began to emit unpleasant smells, as though something within me began to decay. If I looked around me and surveyed my worktable, I thought I knew that it had a host of etchings and among them, like a Trojan horse, an immense number of unbuilt structures that all called themselves Me. So I sat night after night, my ridiculous, fleshless, blue-veined legs crossed, and in my eyes was a burning that the numskulls were attributing to etching acid and printer's ink into which I constantly liked to mix cat's blood. In my groin I felt a tug; crusty places on my elbows were flaking off smolderingly.

I long since had begun to transform myself into an ailment, something rabid—work that was called building. In endless monologues I gave myself roaring sermons and reassured myself that what was artificial created prospects and a future reality. Only the fake work of art lives. He who creates it is dead. Since the door to my cell, which was in reality my work dungeon, had no lock, I always removed the knob and took it with me. In that way, no one could get in, and I knew that I would be undisturbed. I never received visitors in my *boschetto*, into the freedom of which I fled from the constriction of my surroundings, and I lived on no more than bread, olives, and new wine. There I experienced the bleakness of objects and abraded myself on the limits of the universe. On good days I was able to work fourteen or fifteen hours.

I delayed the actual etching as long as possible and tried to envision an etching first and have it all ready in my imagination before I drew its lines with the cold needle. I always began with lines first, but then thought in spaces. As soon as I bent to work over the table and panicked moths buzzed around the lamp, I felt a happy confidence and joyful anticipation, although I knew that the walls of deafness grew thicker and thicker around me. And it was as cold in that room as in a seashell. I was always anxious to create an empty space around me. Then whenever I had completed a work, I felt crushed, exhausted, and lonely. Only once in a while did I go eat at a tavern named *Dal Pompiere* in the Via S. Maria Calderari in the Jewish quarter, where, in order not to be disturbed, I was served in a separate room by a grumpy army sergeant. Even today I am still grateful to the proprietor.

But as soon as dusk fell, I was overcome by a curious unease and fear of the night, as if I were a small child. I swallowed many a bitter medicine brewed of Seneca and the Stoics. For me that was the substitute for a pistol shot. A person is different at night than during the day. With night begins the time of fever, at night miscarried babies and pale women in childbed die, at night victims of liver and kidney colic, asthmatics and those struggling to breathe rave. What I always missed was the good-night kiss and the smile of a human being who, even though I am what I am, loved me in spite of that. Sometimes, then, I stared through a telescope at the stars, murmured their beguiling names like a child's rhyme: Sirius, Orion, Cassiopeia, and saw that God is an animal who wants to flay me. And I lived as chastely as a castrated tomcat. I masturbated. Even Caesar says: *This sweet art is social life for the lonely, a friend for the abandoned, a benefactor for the old man. Even the poorest man is rich, since this majestic diversion is at his bid.* Then again, if I didn't want to become totally bestial and not let my cock discharge cheerlessly under the blanket, I was driven after my nightly blasphemy to the public houses, into the places consecrated to the Venus Cloacina, as the classicists say, to ungainly women whose shifty and calculating lecherousness was not only humiliating but also again shattering. Centuries later I remember this silent trade. *Where grapes hang low, the roguish pluck them,* says the philosopher. Of course, I myself learned one thing in these unutterably depressing places: that the joy of love cannot be formed out of one's own rib, rather that everything is garbage. When, then, with hanging head and fever blisters on my lips I walked back to my galley among whispering bodies, my nocturnal steps gave me the feeling that I was the only one to whom this Rome belonged. These footfalls on the travertine paving in the quiet of this not-yet-awakened day were the music of a shade and were directed by the wind. It lowered the beams of my dungeon down upon me, on which I hung head down with the bats. I already believed that the trees were turning around to me in worn grief and laughing at my defeats, which gathered like scum behind my teeth. While my longing scurried through blue woods, driven by invisible lashes, while I kept regurgitating futility in my ashen mouth and became my own laughter, I recited my dreams to myself like stuttered verses and doing that felt so stricken that I would like to have chased the flowers from the fields. Inside me it looked as dark as inside a fish's mouth. I no longer emerged from this gravel pit of my piteous ludicrousness, of my ludicrous piteousness. In the early morning I screamed at the birds to no longer comfort me, at night I drank my fever out of deep black jugs, every hour I paid my life back at face value with ridiculous desperation. Very often I walked through the nighttime city, when the dead rose out of their coffins, until my wine-filled brain floated up toward the sun. I looked down on the houses with the eyes of strangled birds, mowed down the walls with my glances, and with its shining iron the moon smashed down upon me anew.

Corresponding to my situation, I again took up the *Carceri* because I wanted to burn into the cold soul of the Romans those prisons in which they had stuck me out of their ignorance. They should see the dungeons they had erected, that underground extension of the mamertine prison with its insane perspective of

flights. Besides, Casanova's flight from the leaden chambers of my
hometown of Venice had become known, a depressing story that
I had eagerly received. All of that fit my state of mind very well.
On July 26, 1755, they had arrested the thirty-year-old because of
freemasonry and other ridiculous accusations. The main charge
had never been revealed to him. There was neither a hearing nor
a trial. And Casanova also never found out the verdict. His
*Histoire de ma fuite des prisons de la République de Venise qu'on ap-
pelle Les Plombs* did not appear until years later, *écrité à Dux en
Bohème*, but I already knew about it at the time. Also about the
strangulation apparatus: *The victim is seated with his back to the
wall on which a horseshoe-shaped clamp is fastened, into which his
head is pushed in such a way that the clamp encloses half his neck. A silk
ribbon is put around his neck and led to a winch that is slowly turned
by a torturer and held until the last jerks of the offender die away.*
Casanova's cell measures four by four meters, too low-ceilinged
for him to be able to stand up in it; the heat is murderous, the fleas
a torment, the rats are as big as rabbits. In winter nineteen hours
of deadly darkness prevails with murderous cold. The first effect
of the incarceration under lead roofs is a strong urge to urinate;
the food and drink is more unpleasant than in a family boarding-
house. Casanova must wait for two weeks until, after a few enemas
with barley infusions, he presses out his stone-hard excrement
with terrible pain. In the loft the prisoner finds a pile of old
records of criminal trials from the last century with powerful accusations against all kinds of *finòchios*, mostly in monk's habits.
With particular frequency they are cases of the seduction of vir-
gins in the city's orphanages, among which is also the one whose
inmates daily raised their bell-clear voices in the Church of the
Temptation of Mary not far from the lead chambers at the Riva
degli Schiavoni, voices that flew up to that ceiling painting of

Tiepolo that the artist had completed with his gout-ridden hand shortly after Casanova's imprisonment.

The lead chambers, it says in his memoirs, *are a place where what is false seems true, where reality had to be a dream, a place where the importance of mind is decreased by half, where reason is turned by overheated fantasy into the victim of illusory hope or cruel desperation.*

Inspired by that, one more reason to publish the second edition of the *Carceri* in my own print shop, to lift the twilight and revise the older copperplates, which brought me the contemptuous accusation by the critics of conceited self-quotation. But it was like all of my work: nothing but final stages.

A youthful critic, who presumably achieved undeserved power by all kinds of toadying and intrigues, who, just having with difficulty become a father, made a mint with his pseudo-philosophical condemnations, even drooled in pretended concern *that it was not pleasant to look on and see how here a person, with whom once justified hope was linked, got stuck and wasted his talent in self-smitten repetitions.*

But I opened perspectives into the infinite, darkened the halls and staircases even more, let a labyrinthine damnation appear behind every barred arch and every arcade, deepened the surfaces of shadows, and removed every playful element from earlier sketches. Powerful diagonal hatching emphasized the somberness, gigantic supports overlapped supposed points of rest, vague fogs and veils of mist fell, towers and spiral staircases moved forward in free space, the view to the rear over a dangerous wooden footbridge was unsure, indeterminate surfaces to stand on, quick attempts to sketch views of arches and vaults from below, feverish shortenings of ramps and wall sections were subordinated to a single goal: The enormity of the design was to be a mirror for the enormity of the blame for denying construction to me. Out of that had come a prison for me from which there could be no escape.

That prison was also meant for those who barred me and for critics, but at the same time it was a prison for my ideas. There was no way out: not that every path might have been shut off by bars and barriers, but because this dungeon did not endure a sky above it. When a person knows no way out, then he must put an end to himself. There is no other solution. That's why I extended the perspectives into the distance, that's why I let stairways and flights upward and downward vanish from sight, that's why I pushed spaces toward the observer. Only then would that dungeon be inescapable, in accordance with my will, for the observer.

Even in the *Antichità* the figures were only stenographic reductions of people, insects among insects. Human beings and buildings do not live on the same surface. The world and its inhabitants are not created for one another. Later it was claimed that the horror of the *Carceri* came less from a few mysterious scenes of torture than from the apathy of the human ants that wander around in those immense spaces. The different groups seemed almost never to come into contact with each other or even to be mutually aware of one another's existence, and they certainly never noticed that some of the condemned were being tortured in a dark corner. Perhaps the most oppressive trait of this insignificant crowd was its insensitivity to feelings of vertigo. Those who romped around happily and cheerfully at mind-boggling heights, seemed not to realize that they were moving at the edge of an abyss. That's why, too, what is fantastic about the *Carceri* consists not of a detail but of a thought that is taken to its most extreme consequence. The order of the spaces had a merciless effect—they were built by greater beings and obeyed different laws than we. Of course, they did have a strictly functional effect, but their function was inscrutable.

The *Carceri* are a maze in which neither quiet nor stability can be found anywhere. With them I thought up a system of contradictory illusions that never permits the eye to become accustomed to its surroundings—and, indeed, from the foreground, in which frequently even a framing foothold is lacking, on to the background, where the path opens into uncertainty. I owe this unease to my special etching technique. It operated with a net of lines woven into one another and contradictory cross-hatching in which the orthogonals and diagonals given by architecture were obscured additionally by cast lights and shadows that unfathomably remained. Faintly etched zones were played off against places left totally white, whereby the latter often depict mysterious billows of smoke that veil the hub of the construction and with that take away any point of reference or spatial allusion from the observer. Besides, pulleys, hawsers, gratings, hoists, and supports see to it that the eye is caught in a net of optical traps and wrong tracks. I populated this ambiguous, constantly changing shadow world with only quickly intimated human figures that are placed either standing together in groups at inexplicable activities in the labyrinthine halls or singly, icily isolated. Every sheet of the *Carceri* embodies an endless series of the most horrible possibilities. Nothing is final. Only the darkness. The *Carceri* show the worst possible form of dungeons by making them have the effect of cathedrals, for churches, too, put me in such prisons with their stubborn rejection of my architectural plans. Whoever sees these dungeons must lay aside all hope for liberation and he himself becomes a part of this somberness. He can understand himself only as a prisoner because, through and through, he becomes the inmate of a dungeon, in body and in spirit. The future and the past are extinguished equally in it.

Oh, how much I would have given for the slightest ray of hope in my future!

I experimented on the plates with changing shades of color and various heavy applications of printing ink and in doing so tried to achieve new effects. Occasionally my dungeons seemed like mountains piled up on one another by giants, above which they hoped to take the Olympus of the gods by storm.

I compiled the *Carceri* in eternal memory of the injustice that was done me in not letting me build and to deter eternally such a rampant crime of preventing a creative human being at any price from fulfilling his dreams, and at this opportunity I also recalled Petronius and Seneca, who fell victim to the mania of tyrants bent on banishing art in general from the earth. Square columns and round arches, corbel stones and scrolls, metal fittings on doors and balcony balustrades, vaults of crossed groins and deep stairwells, unsafe steep stairs, wheels of swords at the entrance to the dungeon, chains, torture racks, wooden bridges and ladders were meant altogether to do that. The tiny little figures, those *puppi* with their pompous commotion and their fidgeting gestures, appear unafraid of heights on the highest galleries and the most exposed balustrades, and with indifferent curiosity observe the tortures or, like tourists, form their ant track through the immensities of this architecture but still always resemble the spiritually and morally crippled riffraff that bears the sole blame for the decline of my world. Nowhere should there be a bush, a tree, or even a sprig of grass to be seen.

And those who held me back should recognize something else: that every detail of the gigantic structure had remained standing

as (my) construction site—with prefinished trusses, roof timber-
ing begun, arches and consoles started and made superfluous by
changes in the plan; every other arcade needs struts; between the
abysses of stone, all erected in haste, bridges of wood, balconies of
wood, and wooden booms have to be added later; the stairs and
balustrades either still do not have safety railings or have only one
of them. In the spaces and halls, on the ramps and in the vaults, I
have set up scary-looking instruments that on closer inspection
prove one and all to be the tools of a master architect: hoists, cable
winches, and weight wheels. The wooden stand that I mischie-
vously penetrated with nails is the board cutter, the frightening
pyramid of beams a hoisting apparatus, but the scaffolds are scaf-
folding. The similarity between the instruments of torture and the
technical tools made it possible for me to show the omnipresence
of the executioner and at the same time to symbolize the forced
labor of the architect and the cruel judgment of the clients in not
allowing me to build.

Only for that reason did I increase the number of pendulums
and rope winches, hoists and booms, and made them discernible
as instruments of torture, furnished them with barbed hooks and
spikes, garnished them with chains and cords, and changed them
into torture wheels and Spanish riders. Architectural instruments
are after all nothing but instruments of torture for someone who
is not permitted to build.

But even worse was to come. I was accused of reveling in the
ugly. What humbug! The theory of the fine arts, the legislation of
good taste, the science of aesthetics were already highly developed
and thoroughly refined in my time. Only the concept of the ugly,
although they touched upon it everywhere, had remained behind.
And actually what is ugly exists insofar as what is beautiful does.

What is ugly comes into being from and with the beautiful. It is indignant at what is beautiful and likes to form an alliance with what is comical. In Nature what is ugly exists as little as what is beautiful or straight lines do, and it is a mistake to consider disease as the cause of what is ugly. The realm of the ugly is much larger than the realm of sensual phenomena in general. Beautiful and ugly are not value opposites, rather at best opposites of stimulation. Concerning anything that is ugly it must be said that the relationship to what is beautiful that is negated by it is included. Only what is ugly guarantees the aesthetic correction of tradition.

And again the wind of disaster blew.

My disaster has a great name: Winckelmann!

And they just had to name my century after him, who lived like a camel exclusively on the past. The stray dog of good fortune always licked only his hand and never mine. Our God is so terrible because on the chessboard of the world He is always only on the side of the successful. Winckelmann, that favorite of the mighty. That precocious and smart-alecky beast. That specialist of outward bulge and swelling, house and bed companion of Roman cardinals, styled upward to a figure of John, to the great soul of the German Age of Classicism, monstrosity of nepotism. Celebrated even by Weimar's fiery harlot. More a man of rump than one of head. Become grand through Vatican stall-feeding time, consequently more an ox and ruminant.

The German Winckelmann became the steel trap that tore my life apart. A devil. He had his people everywhere. You should declare *Winckelmann* as a unit of measure for catastrophes of every kind. At the same time this Winckelmann was a person who all his life brilliantly knew how to hide his glaring mediocrity behind his toadying complaisance. Only what was beautiful counted for him: a boy's knee. You should acknowledge this creature only by looking aside.

The greatest misfortune of my life after my wife Angelica came upon me in the figure of this totally unknown German librarian from Nöthnitz near Dresden and his unspeakable writings that treat only of testicles, thighs, and the naked behinds of boys. With that, or just for the sake of that, the German succeeded in forcing all of aesthetics under the shabby Greek yoke and spitting phil-hellenism over all of Europe. The fervor of this guy was not in his head but in his ass.

I know why the Germans, those barbarians necessarily con-trolled by civilization and a rough climate, have been driven to this very day to Italy: homeland on their lips and clubs in their hands. But this Italy has meanwhile declined so far that no one can worry about it anymore. Germans: The creative spirit is more likely something unappetizing to them. Germany is full of junk, and its intellectual life consists of tossing phrases at one another in the gazettes. Winckelmann came from a country where the most upright folk on earth have practiced fidelity and honesty since they rose from the primeval sludge. But in the language of his biographer: *Out of the quiet of Stendal, where Winckelmann grew up as the son of a shoemaker in the most poverty-stricken circum-stances, the path of his life led him through years as a schoolmaster full of hardship and privation to a count's librarianship in Dresden.*

Don't make me laugh!

In solitary hours he succeeded in gaining access to the world of an-tiquity. By converting to Catholicism he saw a way to come closer to his beloved Italy. And in reality he was called to Rome, where he soon rose from level to level and chose as his noble goal the renewal of Hellenism in beauty.

In plain English: This upstart, who as a village schoolteacher felt like a Greek in exile and crammed the *ABC*s into his pupils' scabby heads by himself rattling off similes from Homer, always hung up his small coat neatly according to how the wind was blowing. The German Winckelmann was a weathercock who was even ready for the sake of his career to change his faith like others their shirts. Anyway, he even had his old Hanoverian songbook sent to Rome after him and every morning, for his edification, sang a hymn by his favorite poet Paul Gerhardt: *I sing to thee with heart and mouth, Lord, Light of my Heart.* His fervent reverence for Homer is also ridiculous and embarrassing, for Homer couldn't even write: The *Iliad* and the *Odyssey* originated at a time when poetry was still spread by word of mouth.

This unreliable little man from a German niche came to Rome, like so many of his sort, not as a poor devil like us but right off with a royal fellowship, and he became fanatically enamored of the Eternal City. In a roundabout way his reports, of course, were hardly flattering, when he wrote: *Among things that I miss in Rome is sleep. At night all hell breaks loose. In the great freedom and im-*punité *that prevails here, and with the slovenliness of the police, the yelling, shooting, throwing of firecrackers, and bonfires in all the streets lasts the whole night until dawn. The mob is uncontrolled, and the governor has become tired of having people deported and hanged. Whenever I want to sleep it is necessary to get almost drunk, but that means also is not the best in the unbearable heat.*

That's how those Germans are: The moment they don't like something they call the police and the hangman. But as soon as it involves their career, they dissemble in the most repugnant way. With his affected appearance and his smart-aleck yakking the *stronzo* Winckelmann got ahead immediately as a German would. At first he became the librarian of the state secretary Cardinal Archinto, afterward of Cardinal Albani, and finally the president of Antiquities in the Vatican. And all the while a majority of Germans only pretend to work, act all the while like they are working, and perfect this playacting work so long that they climb to the highest step of the career ladder, while they reproach people like us constantly for laziness and *dolce far niènte*. Germans are possessed only by the fury of production. That has nothing to do with honest work.

But the spider, says Leonardo da Vince in his *Favole*, that believes it has found peace in the keyhole finds death.

It is compromising for an artist whenever he meets a critic. But it is even more compromising when one artist meets another. He ought to change sides of the street immediately.

An encounter with the smooth-shaven and pimply *intriguer* from Stendal—God alone knows where that is located—with that washed-up son of a shoe repairman, could no longer be avoided. I remember the first handshake, received limply with deadly contempt, when I had the feeling of having dipped my hand in a bowl of lukewarm horse piss. I'd rather have torn the look of greed out of his eyes. A naked boy ran out of the room, and with open pants the German asserted: *Je ne suis pas pédéraste.* I had recognized Winckelmann immediately as a *finocchio*, who had more in mind than embracing only the smooth statues of cool marble boys. He constantly talked drivel about *elevation*. What can that mean for someone like that except getting it up?

It's all the same to me whether such a thing is against Nature or not, whether it happens likewise with big-horned sheep, bugs, and macaques. There Winckelmann also followed the ideal of some so-called Greek love as the Socratic model.

In the ninth chapter of the seventh book of his *Memoirs* Casanova reported how he was a witness when Winckelmann, which he always wrote as Vinckelmann—Winckelwife would have been more suitable—fondled the children of the painter Mengs and how the false abbot admits what is in reality concealed behind his philhellenism: *Dans mes longue études, je suis devenu d'abord l'admirateur, puis l'adorateur des anciens, qui comme vous savez ont presque tous été b . . . sans s'en cacher, et plusieus d'entre eux immortalisant par leurs poèmes les gentils objets de leur tendresse, et même par des monuments superbes.*

Winckelmann's talk that he had a Greek in him who most ardently wanted to achieve knowledge of what beauty is was revolting. The shoemaker's son was always just lecherous about boys. Whenever with affected daintiness and simulated grace he asked about places *which Apollo honored with his presence,* in reality he meant male prostitutes and pardoned himself with the comment that beauty was pure, without color and taste like perfect spring water. When his hands lewdly stroked marble thighs, he called sculpture the most exquisite sensuousness: *Stone becomes flesh and both eternity.* In addition he spoke his Saxon dialect unendurably. His words hung like lead weights on his terrible Saxon speech. He spoke it until he was blue in the face, and dribble spattered around the corners of his mouth, madness dripped in his eyes. Thought quickly becomes lame under the degrading burden of this Saxon language, which makes everything thought of implausible and impossible even before it is expressed. When he spoke in his sluggish way, he always opened up his mouth too widely so that the words spewed out like slime. Besides, he stank constantly of garlic and cold semen.

Of course, through dull industry he acquired some knowledge of ancient artworks by reading up on them, but his fatuous *History of the Art of Antiquity,* supposedly the first work in the German language on art theory, made him famous. With the pathos of anticipation and revelation the ambitious man inquired into historical grandeur and propagated the knowledge of great princes, clever heroes, and strong spirits. With his cleaned-up chatter

Winckelmann belonged to those scribblers who filled paper for money and fame. Therein lay a great swindle, for anything worth writing about is written about by someone who writes for the sake of a subject. The whole trouble with literature today is that everyone who wants to be famous writes a book. The public is stupid enough to buy it, and the reviewers cheer such cannon fodder. Most authors today write without thinking. Then there are authors who think while they are writing, and finally those who have thought before they write. They are extremely rare. *All over the world*, says the philosopher, *rules are turd droppings.*

For this particular Winckelmann the pen was to thinking what, for the cripple, the cane is to walking. But the most elegant and easiest walking is that without crutches. Winckelmann's scribbling shows with every word how an empty head tries to help an empty moneybag. In reality this *stronzetto* simply had nothing to say. The banality of his squeezed-out gray matter can be measured in the fact that his fancy intellect couldn't understand the meaning of his own sentences at all. So his sentences walk around constantly on stilts. Just as the guy had constantly to spruce himself up, that's how pretentious his language is. Since the phony didn't know what he wanted to say, he expressed himself quite solemnly, mysteriously, or enigmatically in order to have the greatest possible interesting and intelligent effect. The swine tried to hide his lack of ideas in a flood of words. Truth is most beautiful unadorned, says the philosopher. But it is violated by bombast, the tone of superiority, and exclusivity. In addition there is his bad habit of joining sentences crosswise and nailing them mutually on the cross because five things are supposed to be said at the same time. Supposedly that's connected to the general ponderousness of the Germans, which gives itself away in their hustle and bustle and above all in their annoying preference for intricately involved and screwed-up sentences. It's there, in bombast and in affected refinement, that they are most pleased with themselves. Winckelmann's sentence structures resemble stuffed geese. And at the same time they are really nebulous, as though their unhappy author would like to leave a back door open through which he can slip away unnoticed. Germans consider this obtuseness as a sign of genius to this very day.

I have never been able to accept this supposedly very significant work, this incredible knavish trick.

Because of this unfortunate German, the line of sight was turned from Roman to Greek antiquity, whose essence he sought to comprehend as *noble simplicity and quiet grandeur in stance as well as in expression.*

For good reason I really should remain silent about Winckelmann's murder in Trieste. But now it doesn't matter anymore. For me, as a Venetian, only Trieste was possible as a place of vengeance. Trieste is the last city in the world, says its most important poet. Of all places, Trieste, famous for its *Regolamento contro il fuoco*. Of all places, Trieste, with its ridiculous Canal Grande, since 1719 elevated by the Austrian Charles VI to a free harbor and as a rival to Venice. Of all places, Trieste, that petit-Vienna on the Adriatic, that place of weary white-haired old people, that pensionopolis, that gerontocracy, in which these days three times as many are buried as are born. Of all places, Trieste, the city of assassins, where Guglielmo Oberdan helped throw a bomb at Emperor Francis Joseph I, whom he didn't hit but with which he brought himself to the gallows. Of all places, Trieste, on the margin of peoples, where even the dumbest comes to the world with four languages and where a metaphysical ache slumbers in every merchant. In that city of anachronistic grace and threadbare *grandezza* there is a bronze angel, it is said, that takes the life of travelers. Mean tongues never wearied of insisting, of course, that my hands played a role in that killing—it had been a real execution—for everyone knew how much I envied Winckelmann and how I had hated him with every fiber of my being. But no court in the world will ever be able to prove anything about me. Also, the report of the Trieste jurist Domenico de Rossetti, which did not appear until 1818, half a century after

Winckelmann's death, doesn't mention me with a single word.

The murderer was named Francesco Arcangeli and was a kitchen helper from Campiglio near Pistoia, with frequent previous convictions and expelled from the land, although exceedingly well built and yet with the face of a girl. He was that cook of whom my friend Marchi had spoken. Some suspected that Arcangeli was a hired *bravo* of the Holy Office, about which the *cazzo* Winckelmann had reported not exactly with flattery in his private letters—others thought him one of those handsome boys that Winckelmann could not leave alone. Concerning which, the daring view also cropped up that I had used the homoerotic inclination of my opponent and hired Arcangeli.

Admittedly, this idea does make some sense. It could certainly have happened that way. But no one in the world will ever be able to prove an iota about it in regard to me. Remarkably, Winckelmann's relationship to Arcangeli is striking: Just imagine a previously convicted young hustler next to a man who was accustomed to move among cardinals, rulers, and scholars important in Europe, who had just been received and honored by Empress Maria Theresa, who corresponded with princes and potentates, and who had negotiated with Frederick the Great about a position at the Prussian court.

I knew only too well about Winckelmann's passions, which he had striven so unsuccessfully to keep secret. You had only to look at the guy, how he moved and how hungrily he circled those beautiful boys, who these days would be doing underwear commercials.

Noble simplicity and quiet grandeur.

I know what he was thinking about when he fashioned those ludicrous words. Certainly not of the harmony of a statue, rather much more of that breech presentation that the better society or Rome always arrogated to itself as a particularly attractive privilege.

Besides, I know from a reliable source what had happened shortly before the murder, for I never lost that Teutonic shoemaker's son from my sight.

On April 10, 1768, Winckelmann left Rome in the company of the sculptor and art dealer Bartolomeo Cavaceppi (whom, by the way, I know very well), seized by a wild longing to see his fatherland once more. At the same time, Germany's best was visiting the archaeologist and Antiquario della Camera Apostolica, member of the St. Luke's Academy, the Accademia Etrusca, and a few other scholarly societies in Rome.

I had heard about the travel plans and was really relieved to know that the Eternal City was finally rid of that fop. According to the reports of Cavaceppi, the trip as far as South Tirol took place without incident. In South Tirol the German had been seized by a melancholia typical of his Teutonic character, which in the jargon of the time was still called *down in the dumps* and which in the further course of the journey past Munich and Augsburg had intensified into an insurmountable loathing of German landscapes and methods of building. Perhaps the true reason also lay in the rejection of Fridericus Rex, who had answered the false abbot that his demands for an honorarium were *trop pour un Allemand.* Previously Winckelmann had called him a divine monarch, for whom he was filled with worshipful respect. Since the beginning of the Seven Years' War he apostrophized him as a *distruttore del genere umano* and *tiranno scellerato,* before he discovered his Prussian heart again, after the war was won. Winckelmann, the mental louse. Always in a Pindaric high tone off the beaten path.

Bartolomeo Cavaceppi, who had started a collection of ancient sculptured feet, was, with his coarse and robust ways, never a friend of what was German. An artist between a stonemason and

a sculptor, he knew how to make himself heard and respected, especially as he was a good businessman. His trade grew, and especially the German princes, among them the king of Prussia, gave
him a lot of business. Anyway, Cavaceppi was also once involved
in a knifing incident. The causes were never wholly clarified, but
everyone knew that he could wield a good blade. Cavaceppi
gained Winckelmann's attention when he passed a few handsome
lads to him, who posed as models for him and whom the German,
because of their hips, the play of muscles, and the dangling between their legs, at once thought of as demigods.

Winckelmann had decided, Cavaceppi later said, to return to
Italy. Only, he wanted to make a stop at the Viennese court, for he
was vain and knew that they would seek his favor and esteem him
there. He did, indeed, reject a tempting offer from Maria Theresa,
but he did not turn down the silver and gold commemorative
coins. There were more than eighty in one silken pouch, in another about fifteen ducats, a gold watch, gold rings and buttons,
and various letters of credit in addition. He was always like that:
coquettish and greedy for money at the same time.

Those very things were to become his undoing. Before he could
start his return trip to the south, plagued by anxieties and full of
inner doubt about his work up to that time, he was laid low by a
mysterious fever. On May 28 he started out for Trieste, on June 1
he arrived at the Adriatic. On the day of his arrival Winckelmann
got acquainted in the hotel with his murderer Arcangeli. The
popular tongue tells the truth: There is in this city an archangel
who takes the life of such travelers.

Thus it was planned, and so it happened.

Arcangeli at once makes himself indispensable to him and
is helpful to him in getting passage on a ship to Ancona.

Winckelmann seems generous and companionable, as is the way of Germans abroad: entirely a man of the world and full of euphoria at soon being again in his beloved South. He calls himself Giovanni Neos, and Arcangeli assures the German he will guard his incognito. But the nimble-minded Tuscan knows how to tempt the aesthete: with the latter's vanity. The *stronzo* Winckelmann falls for the flattery and finally shows Arcangeli those valuable coins that had been given to him by the Austrian empress.

Arcangeli knew that they would be his reward after the deed was done, for the one who had hired him and whose name will never come to light, had promised them to him with a few gold pieces into the bargain. Of course, before the court the murderer is clever enough to conjure up a totally different explanation out of his hat, and he swears a Sicilian oath:

Since, on the basis of Winckelmann's conversation, the opinion took root in me that he was some kind of Lutheran, Jew, or spy and a completely useless person with an abnormal penchant for his own sex, I decided to carry out my plan. Winckelmann never wanted to go with me into a church or to mass; when he passed by a church, he did not remove his hat. And often he read in a large book that was neither German nor French nor Italian but was printed in another language that I did not know. So I considered it a heretical work of an occult doctrine, which turned out to be a Greek edition of Homer.

A clever rascal and an intelligent Italian, Arcangeli was able to withhold the name of his client adroitly, for after all, on the basis of excellent connections to the better society of Rome and, above all, to the Vatican, he could hope that sooner or later by way of a covert hostile act or a political gambit his client would free him from prison.

So the legend of robbery and murder with a homoerotic background was born and at once believed, especially since Arcangeli had left no doubt with the judges about how very much the German had also pressed him sexually and how often he himself had had to resist such testicular fondling in public. The chambermaid Serafina, likewise let in on the secret, was questioned insufficiently by the court and in that way didn't even have to lie. The whole incident seemed to me like a perfectly staged theatrical piece: a comedy with a fatal outcome. And I was triumphant, for the murderer never revealed the name of his client. Even if he had done that, no one would have believed him. There were neither witnesses nor proof.

During his journey the vain German "boy" had fallen for a young female tightrope walker named Bice in a Krainian village, who sleeping and dancing embodied the concept of ancient harmony and grace, and in whom he believed he had found the living image of beauty. But the girl was in reality a boy—sought after and bribed by an expert on the theory of proportions—who had the task of causing a certain heat to rise in Winckelmann. The German performer of genius, Goethe, who was likewise lured to my country, knew about that passion when he wrote: *So we often find Winckelmann in a relationship with handsome youths, and he never seems more lively.*

There's only one thing I don't understand: Why that gentleman from Weimar had to eulogize his effeminate countryman in such an enormously hypocritical way: *He lived as a man and he passed on as a perfect man. From his grave the aura of his power strengthens us and awakens in us the liveliest urge with zeal and love to continue on and forever with what he began.*

Winckelmann's last will and testament gives us no insights about the background of his murder. Heirs are the Cardinal

Albani, whom Winckelmann had once described as a *stupid fizzy wind*, the copperplate engraver Mogalli, an unimportant man who was to leave no trace in the history of our art, the musician Annibali, of which something similar can be said, and the fund for the poor of Trieste.

It always cheered me in my deepest core that the devil Winckelmann in his last hour was surrounded by, of all things, the angelic names Serafina and Arcangeli. For I knew from my dissolute wife Angelica what is hidden behind such angelic names. And my father, who had committed the crime of siring me, was named Angelo.

Officially, the German's name never passed my lips, and you will look for him in vain even in my polemical pamphlets. You cannot imagine how even the way of walking and the affected behavior of this spoiled upstart sent me into a frenzy. But beyond those things he also had the cheek to bring his confused viewpoints into the world and draw all the influential personalities to his side because in their narrow-mindedness they had nothing from their own intellectual accomplishments to counter the deception wrought by the vain German fop in priestly robes.

And all the while, I had made it so easy for them with my writings—they needed only to read them. The table was richly set. They just had to dig in. But reading must be learned. Not everyone can do it. How much knowledge of the divine escapes understanding because proper reading is lacking?

In my essay *Della Magnificenza ed Architettura de'Romani* I thought, first of all, of a theoretical treatise, to a certain extent a summation of my studies and insights up to then. Besides, I took counsel with classicists such as Clemente Orlandi, Monsignore Bottari, and Pater Contucci. Stupendous erudition distinguished my expositions. But it was this very thing that put most readers' noses out of joint: Small-minded people couldn't follow me, talked about peculiar ideas, and accused me of hotheadedness and intolerance.

From my colleagues in the French Academy I knew about the famous *Querelle des Anciens et des Modernes,* in which it was also a matter of the primacy of Greek over Roman.

And then this German came along, crept under the soutanes of papal court toadies and underhanded diplomats, and the philhellenists made their arrival into the Eternal City with him. They had just praised my meticulousness and applauded Roman grandeur, they had just seen architecture as the peak of all art and culture, and then in the European discussion about the preeminence of Greek ahead of Roman art I was pushed to the edge with my views, laughed at, and accused of fantastic monumentalism. I could have gotten over the laughter, since in the meantime I was used to it. But most detestable was that sympathetically amused pat on the back in front of all those who yesterday would most liked to have crawled away from me to somewhere else.

The scene of intellectual disputes moved away from architecture to—it's a shame to even say it—to reliefs on sarcophagi, vases, cameos, statues, and other trivialities. Suddenly—how ridiculous—the human figure was the measure of beauty. Meanwhile, the representatives of this perverse theory had only to look once in the mirror themselves to see what lunacy they had advocated. And in architecture only the harmony of proportions should count.

Noble simplicity and quiet grandeur.

Again and again that unendurable *basso continuo* with the brutality of a mendacious headline, that Grecian buffoonery with which the harmony-addicted Winckelmann beautified everything, smoothed out the contradictions and, like a professor, simply lied his way past whatever he didn't like. That could also have come from the mouth of my pretty, dumb Angelica, who, to top it all, also imagined she had to engage and take part in clever conversations whenever among men I led a public conversation with a few experts. What silly Winckelmann-Winckelwife chatter.

On the other hand, I always had exalted firmness *(firmitas)*, utility *(utilitas)*, and beauty *(venustas)* as the prerequisites of architecture. And in this regard I knew I was in agreement with Vitruvius and Palladio. But how quickly is one pushed aside, how quickly one becomes a loser. Yesterday they had still been kissing my feet, today they wanted to stone me, called my comments a mixed-up pile of misunderstood arguments, and suggested cynically to me that I return to my shoemaker's last, which up to this time they had so stubbornly denied me.

Of greatest trouble was a conjurer and soldier of fortune named Julien-David Le Roy, a miserable and arrogant Frenchman, who—like that unspeakable German—had for a time been a fellowship holder in Rome and had used a negligently short stay in Greece to turn into money a highly superficial image of the ruins of Corinth, Athens, and Attica with hastily thrown together measurements, error-ridden cracks, but adorned with commercially appealing descriptions—the botched-up job was called *Les Ruines des plus beaux monuments de la Grèce.*

Everyone rushed to buy that new book and made its author a rich man overnight. Le Roy scrupulously made use of public discussion, exaggerated the significance of what was Greek that had become popular, and with his scribbles he won undeserved influence and respect. When I replied angrily to that and proved he made the silliest mistakes, fielded my archaeological as well as my architectonic knowledge against that deception by a charlatan, and prepared a devastating rebuff, I had long since lost the favor of the public.

They did not reproach Le Roy for his flagrant blunders but said of me that I had gotten hopelessly entangled in my own well-laid traps. I was finished. They had not only not let me build but now also made my graphic works, which I had prepared not least in praise of the Roman architecture of antiquity, a laughing stock of the town. Still, I single-mindedly continued to sing the praise of the *fermezza,* for building mass and indestructibility are the first commandments of architectonic mastery. Only the power of the forces of Nature or the destructive work of time could lay a hand on these monuments. *Fermezza* lets artistic thoughts continue to be effective. Even the formless heaps of rubble and projection of walls, even the broken stumps of columns and exposed foundations carried the *fermezza* into the present for me. Putting utilitarian structures into the same category with cult buildings was interpreted as sheer heresy. But for me, the holy shrine of Jupiter on the Capitol and the Cloaca Maxima were not antithetical.

I was far more concerned with a liberation of aesthetics from the canon of high rank and style. My praise of the Roman sewer system infuriated the admirers of Greek elegance and refinement. I found agreement only from Carlo Lodoli, a Venetian padre and extreme outsider, who in long-standing and exhausting lecture tours had presented his theory of strict functionality of every building with the zeal of a sectarian. But his opinion had long since stopped being taken seriously. I came across more and more proofs against the popular mimicking admiration of what was Greek in studying Pliny the Elder, who after all mentioned the architectonic accomplishments of Roman emperors, the extent and significance of which did not have to take second place to the building of the pyramids. Finally, the criticism by the public tried to finish me off. Instead of my own writings, people read only the repulsive scribblings of the critics in some bickering sheet or other and spread the deadly mantle of silence like a glassy catafalque over my reponses. They buried me alive.

To this very day the criticism of me has something so silly about it that I'm sorry to have mentioned it. Again and again the arbiters of art had applied their surveyor's pole like drunken journeymen masons. They claim to be judges of art. But they would have to reach that art first. Art is aristocratic. It is the negation of equality and what is vulgar, a glorification of the unique and extraordinary, of personality and individuality. Its intransigence has its basis in the fact that in art the individual, the single human being, expresses himself. These days there is an outcry on all sides for the grandiose financing of art. The result is a mountain that gives birth to a mouse and produces nothing but drivel. Of course, critics talk about themes that they do not master and call themselves experts. They claim to assess style and are themselves the greatest parody of style. They claim to be teachers and educators, as though art were a school essay to which the guru had only to add a grade. But art is indigestible, stays stuck in your craw, is a swallowed fish bone in the gullet of the mighty. Critics despised my quirks, I their cowardice and their stupidity that screamed to high heaven. *I'd like to have just a millimeter of the nerve that all those guys with the sense of honor of rats have. It's their chief organ. There is nothing underneath it.* Why must they, like predators, sink their teeth in every chunk of an artist's flesh, just to gnaw around on it and finally to tear it to bits. The critic's sole miserable joy and hubris consists of plunging a knife into the back of the artist, of raking the fame of his criticism, and wanting to have the sympathy of his victim to boot. The most prominent characteristics of critics are ambition (to be better than the artist), vanity (of being an artist themselves), and envy (of the artist): melted all together in shamelessness and insolence. Dirt always floats to the top. For was there ever a single comment on my works that I would not have had to retract in an instant on the grounds alone of hair-raising objective errors that are obvious to any beginner? But why do I refer to objective argumentation, where, for critics, it is after all a matter of a lack of objectivity. In this regard they try incessantly to exceed one another, and no baseness is too slight for them. The honor of an artist does not depend upon what he does but on what he suffers. But critics are the ones who sunder his honor. With their quick recommendations and rash executions the critics show only how little they do know in ever being sure of their judgments. After all, a Roman maxim goes: *Non è si tristo cane, che non meni la coda.* No dog is so mean that it doesn't wag its tail. An artist doesn't need a critic because, if he's really an artist, he is himself his harshest critic. And for an architect, time is the only judge. In actuality, the critic has exclusively a duty to be helpful. If he does not recognize that duty, rather merely deviates from the artwork, lets his ideas about art dominate, and judges the quality of an artwork by this mostly strange idea, the critic misses his real duty and does not mediate between an artwork and a public but disturbs and destroys that relationship.

After I had been dragged through the cloaca of gazettes, academies, salons, and conference halls, I turned defiantly to the study of the Cloaca Maxima. And from there reached back to a plan I had set aside: my book about the Field of Mars. For me it was nothing less than a repetition of the unrepeatable, a reconstruction of the Campus Martius in its old glory: a labyrinth of intertwined temples and theaters, halls of honor and baths, libraries and arsenals, an interplay of concave and convex lines of ground plans, put together out of triangles, trapezoids, and rhombuses. I wanted to document my open break with the feminine laws of noble simplicity and quiet grandeur. My imagination had to let off steam again in a new free space in dizzying multiplicity. A new procedure had to be tested: the imaginary exposure of ruins overbuilt, alienated to the senses and covered by the trash of history.

In a long series of elaborately executed landscapes I tried to illustrate the still existing ruins of the Campus Martius and its building components that I had reconstructed but not made visible. In addition I first of all peeled the ruins out of their later sheaths and then lowered the ground to the level of the age of the Roman emperors. I wanted to outdo myself in the detailed structure of the devastated beauty of these ruins and unsparingly remove two thousand years of Roman history, for ruins are dead and immortal at the same time. Hands worked on them that speak a different language, that speak my language.

The horror that I drew lay in the material, in the ruins, which were to express the relationship of the material to human beings.

I knew I *had* to build.

Again I etched my open wounds, again I transferred my desperate accusation onto the copperplate. With my plan of the Campus Martius and with the contrasting skeleton appearance of the ancient ruins I went on my way to the end of what was possible for me.

And so after the grant of the papal license, in my letter of dedication to Robert Adam, who had somewhat reluctantly presented himself as a patron, I wrote:

I can assure you that for me no part of the Campus was too unimportant to be repeatedly and thoroughly investigated. I pressed even into the cellars of the houses—not without trouble and cost—just in case a small detail might escape me. When I had collected the remnants of the buildings and had copied them with great care, I compared them with the old plan of the city on the Capitol with the hope that in this case no one could maintain I had followed more my own caprice rather than reliable argumentation and probable conjecture in the captions, the exterior shape, and the topographical arrangement of the monuments. Unfortunately, I fear that some of the areas of the Campus described could be held as monstrosities of my power of imagination that can in no way be supported by proof. And indeed, anyone who compares them with the architectural theory of the ancients must determine that they deviate very strongly from it and are far more closely related to the architectural modes of our own time. Perhaps it is the unavoidable and general law that the arts, after they have achieved their bloom, must decay, but perhaps it lies in the nature of man, in his artistic skills as well as in all other things, to demand some latitudes for himself.

Severely shaken, but defiant and single-minded, I kept working—and my contemporaries took my zeal for pathological obsession. All the humiliations gave me no peace. I still wanted to prove what I had in me.

No slacking, I told myself, don't give up. Put up with the derision, the mockery. Art degenerates when the artist begins to fail to endure derision and mockery. Everybody has declared that I am crazy, but I had to accept that, for genius always lives one floor above madness. I've accepted it the whole time, for the true artist has to be consistent in the madness of his art, and he deserves to be called a true artist only when he has plunged unconditionally into the madness of his art. But I have madness behind me already.

When I had finally realized that, I had a presentiment that I would still have to sleep over for several more centuries. I have, so to speak, only spent the night all these centuries.

Soon I traveled to Lago di Albano, then to Lago Fucino, then again to Castel Gandolfo on behalf of the pope. No stone was too insignificant for me, I omitted no suspicious hole, I measured thousands of details, took on wearisome test borings and dangerous excursions into forgotten channels, and did not ignore the testimonials of Latin architecture in Etruscan Cora. Work was the bitterest and at the same time the best medicine.

Three other publications by me appeared, abundant with footnotes and comments. Their disadvantage consisted only in that they assumed too much knowledge and a thorough study of traditions.

I went my way alone, locked windows and doors, retreated to my library, read, as much as I could stand, no longer read the writings but devoured them and finally discovered that books are the most loyal companions and in any case are superior to people. Occasionally art has more compassion than people do. In addition, the books taught me that people are allowed a kind of pride, the pride of one who in the darkness of the world around him does not give up and permits no one to penetrate his dreams. In that darkness words weigh double, and many a sentence releases its venom only years later.

With this knowledge I roved through the centuries. I have met countless people, but I seldom responded to them. Occasionally someone reported meeting me and did not stick to the advice that reads: *Anyone who writes about the dead, the undead of the eighteenth century, then runs the risk of making a mistake by spending his life writing.* The best example of that is a Russian named Odojevski:

The only window through which my soul looks into the world of poetry is bibliomania: my passion. Otherwise, a man also like any other, I am transformed as soon as books are involved. For their sake I went throughout Europe. Besides, like all bibliophiles, I am extraordinarily stingy. This condition made me avoid public auctions, where as a bibliophile you can come to ruin worse than by playing cards. Instead, I zealously visited the small shops, where I spent little but had the satisfaction of rummaging through absolutely all of them. Bibliomania is one of the strongest passions when given full rein, and I completely understand anyone whom it leads to murder. In the year 1844 I was drawn by it to Italy. In Naples, to my great regret, I found at first little opportunity to indulge my passion. I was all the more delighted when on a stroll over the Piazza Nova I finally found an antiquarian bookshop. With all the cunning of a bibliophile I approached the bookshop indifferently, and while I leafed with concealed impatience in old prayer books, I at first did not notice that in the other corner a figure in an old-fashioned French jacket and with a powdered wig, under which a carefully woven hairnet hung, had stepped up to a large folio. I don't know what caused each of us to turn around. In that figure I recognized that eccentric who in the same clothing always strolled around with dignity in Naples and at every meeting, especially with ladies, doffed his worn-out three-cornered hat with a smile. I had seen this character a long time before, and I was absolutely delighted at the opportunity of making his acquaintance. I glanced at the book open in front of him: It was a collection of badly printed etchings of architectural edifices. He was studying it with close attention, with his fingers took the measure of the colored columns, laid a finger on his brow and sank into deep reflection. Obviously he is an architect, I thought, and to please him I will claim to be an admirer of architecture. My gaze fell on a collection of enormous folios with the title Opere del Cavaliere Giambattista Piranesi: *Excellent! I thought, took a volume, opened it; but the depicted sketches in it of immense projects of enormous structures, every one of which would have gobbled up millions and entire centuries, those sculptured boulders moved to mountain tops, those rivers transformed into fountains—all of that captivated me so much that for a moment I forgot the eccentric. The strongest impression was made on me by a volume that, almost from the beginning to the end, was filled with depictions of prisons of various kinds; there were endless vaults, bottomless holes, palaces, chains, walls overgrown with grass and, as embellishment, every kind of execution and torture that the criminal imagination of man had ever conceived. I was so fascinated by the book that I felt the need to share my enthusiasm with the next-best person. So I turned to the eccentric, who was sunken in his reading. The man faced up to me indignantly with the expression of a person who is annoyed at being disturbed at his preoccupation with an important matter. But hardly had he cast a glance at the book I had opened up than he recoiled with horror, waved his hands about in the air, and cried out: "Close it, for God's sake, close that useless, that frightful book!" "But no!" I answered. "I like it so much that I'm going to buy it," and I pulled out my purse. "Money," the eccentric whispered, "you have money!" And his whole body trembled. "Do you need a little? Perhaps I can help you out," I said, for somehow I felt sorry for the man in his theatrical condition between megalomania and terror. "Money? Of course I need*

money," the old man said, "for a start a little would have been of help
to me—really, no more than a little: ten million." I couldn't help laughing and asked why he had need of that enormous sum. "To build a
vault that would connect Ætna and Vesuvius, and for the arch of triumph that should be at the entrance to the park of the palace I projected." I could only shake my head and lend expression to my
astonishment about why a person with such gigantic plans had spoken
with such disdain about the book that I had just been about to show
him. Their ideas were not at all so distant from his own. "Not at all so
distant?" the stranger exclaimed, "not at all so distant! Why do you
come at me again with this damned book, when I'm its author!" A cold
shudder ran down my back. "No, that's going too far," I answered, and
with that I grabbed the Historical Dictionary that happened to be
lying nearby and showed him the page on which was printed:
"Giambattista Piranesi, Italian copperplate engraver, archaeologist,
and master builder . . . died 1778." "That's nonsense! Lies! Nothing but
lies!" the eccentric shouted. "Oh, how happy I would be, if it were true!
But I'm alive, and the days go past without a sound, hot, heavy, one
after the other sinking into the past as though into an abyss. The rings
of the years lie strangling about my heart. To my own misfortune, I'm
alive—and this damned book won't let me die. If you knew how old I
am according to the calendar, you would be appalled." My curiosity
grew by the minute. "Explain this strange phenomenon to me," I said
very quietly to him, "entrust me with your sorrow: I repeat, perhaps I
can help you." The eccentric's features brightened. He grabbed my hand.
"I would particularly like to warn you about me, Sir. You see, I tell stories, I'm a fabulist. You don't know what that means? Well, there are
mutants, vagabonds, ignoramuses, pretenders, defrauders, flagellants,
troublemakers—all that taken together makes a fabulist. A genuine
fabulist is someone who stares into the terrible face of futility. I want to

*tell you the story of my life. But afterward, don't say that I had not ex-
pressly warned you about me. Just don't say that!" And the eccentric told
me the terrible ridiculous miserable story of his life gone wrong. He
closed with the words: ". . . in vain, all in vain. Now you know my
misfortune. Help me, as you promised me. Only ten million. I beg you!"
And with those words the unfortunate man fell onto his knees before
me. Full of astonishment and compassion I looked at the poor man, took
a ducat, and said: "That's all that I can give you now." The old man
looked at me despondently. "I knew it," he replied, "a pittance. But that,
too, is all right. I'll add it to the sum that I'm collecting to buy Mont
Blanc and level it to the ground—because otherwise it will block the
view from my pleasure palace." And with those words the old man left
hurriedly and disappeared into the crowd.*

In Livy, I came upon the prophecy that the Romans could hope
for the collapse of the city of Veii only if they succeeded before-
hand in lowering the level of Lake Albano. Thereupon the
Romans are said to have built an artificial drain of the lake by digging a tunnel almost as tall as a man through the cliffs around the
mountain lake. That idea fascinated me, and I wanted to test the
truthfulness of it, completed anew sketches of the location, cross
sections of the landscape, expensive construction models and dia-
grams: *Descrizione e disegno dell'Emissario del Lago Albano.*

I inspected the entrance to the tunnel. To figure out how the
work was done, I had a fisherman enter the space of the channel
with a torch in his hand, whereupon I instructed him to press on
as far inside as the water permitted. You see, usually the water
stands five handbreadths deep, in certain years, however, only two
handbreadths deep; and in the year 1762 I found exactly two
handbreadths and the same in the year before. Now when I had
the fisherman enter the channel, I cautioned him to observe care-

fully whether he might encounter a meeting of a shaft with the channel. The fisherman went inside as far as he could and reported to me that after a long stretch he had found the ceiling of the channel open and a creepy empty space vertically above, quadrangular and much broader than the channel. I don't have to say that this excavation was one of the shafts that I was looking for! So I had the fisherman press forward once more to the same location with a thin rope, which he tied together several times, in order to measure the distance from it to the beginning of the outlet. Afterward, I began to investigate another shaft, and finally it was clear to me that the ancients could have dug out the channel in no other way than I had assumed in my drawings. The landscapes that I created were pure night pieces, as they appealed to my temperament: underground ashlar landscapes, hardly illuminated by a sideways beam of light or one falling from above, the masonry of cyclopean character, as though it did not support the tunnel against the massive rock, rather was its substructure. As long as night drags itself laboriously up a mountain, we see better into what has gone missing in the past than by day.

On the occasion of my study Di due *Spelonche ornate dagli antichi alla riva del Lago Albano* I discovered that the almost lightless caves and grottoes had once been the scene for the orgies of Publius Clodius Pulcher, which Cicero had scourged so indignantly. But my demeanor and my clothes were so suspicious to the natives that they thought me a heretic and wanted to slay me on the spot. Again the wind of misfortune enveloped me. Only with great difficulty did I succeed in escaping their assaults. Doubtless these numskulls had been incited by my opponents, who didn't want to stand for it that I, still in service to the pope, had been commissioned to capture in their entirety the antiquities in the area surrounding the papal summer residence of Castel Gandolfo.

Once I laid my etchings and sketches before the pope, and he asked me how many of them I still had in mind to produce. His gallery was fairly full of them already.

"That depends on Your Holiness," I replied. "Command me! A sheet is as easy for me to produce as a blessing is for you."

After the Roman antiquities I now wanted to research the Etruscan ones and set out for Cora, an old Etruscan city southeast of Velletri. The towering city wall, built of polygonal blocks of stone, and the vestibule of the Temple of Hercules with Doric entablatures in elegant overrefinement, supported my thesis of the independent development of the art of the Latins and the autonomy of their aesthetic sensibilities even where geographical proximity to the Greeks might have suggested a submission to foreign tastes. But my etchings were dealt with more openly and with harsher criticism: The pervasion of what was real and what was visionary was more and more unbridled, the sublime raised more and more to a fata morgana and to the fabulous. The reproaches and the personal charges of scholars who do nothing but sit out their university positions became more vehement and shameless. I was accused in all seriousness of having in mind only what was theatrical; travelers could no longer rely on the representations I had made; I was distancing myself as an artist and archaeologist from my contemporaries; my increasing eccentricity, the shrieks of my humiliated soul, to which construction was denied, had to be raised as arguments against me. In the long run none of my co-workers were ready to submit to my supposedly wondrous theories and excesses.

And again the wind of misfortune blew.
In the year 1764, when the marquise de Pompadour died and
Kant was proceeding with his *Observations on the Feeling of the
Beautiful and the Sublime,* there appeared in the *Gazette Littéraire
de l'Europe* a letter by the critic Jean Pierre Mariette, which tried
to deal me a sharp rebuff intended to condemn me—from the
standpoint of fashionably progressive philhellenism, didactically
disparaging me and my work in an arrogant tone, but in particular arguing rather superficially.

A rigged game, which left me standing there like a fool com-
piling the proofs against himself. The blasphemous writing was
shot through with the Winckelmannian tone I found so repulsive;
it just teemed with *belle et noble simplicité.*

Again I was caught in a maelstrom of misfortune, from which
I was never supposed to escape. Long nights whirled past in alco-
holic fog, for when I drank I started to feel sober. I reeled through
a darkened mind of hallucinations and dread, in a very short time
lost weight heavily, was just skin and bones, looked like a
wretched, emaciated spindle and was yet a ravenous maw. The
wrinkles around my mouth and eyes had turned into deep furrows. I felt as though someone had stuck a stiletto in the hollows
of my knees, and I made a big mistake: I reacted on the spot.

My *Osservazioni di GioBattista Piranesi sopra la Lettre de M.
Mariette aux Auteurs de la Gazette Littéraire de l'Europe, Inserita nel*

Supplemento dell'istessa Gazzetta stampata Dimanche 4. Novembre MDCCLIV consists of three parts: first the reprint of Mariette's epistle with a comprehensive commentary, second a dialogue about the principles of architecture—the *Parere su L'Archittetura*—and third the introduction to the planned tractate *Della introduzione e del progresso delle belle arti in Europa ne'tempi antichi*. The sentence-by-sentence refutation of Mariette's account was so successful for me because it consists of the unproven arbitrariness of his assertions about the Greek origin of the Etruscans and of the paucity of proofs. I merely had to quote my old, indefatigably repeated arguments. In my testimonial about architecture, the second part, two experts, a supporter and an opponent of my position, converse about some recent bizarre architectural drawings. The accuser, Protopiro, complains about my chaos and accuses me of having indulged in mad arbitrariness and my own whims with disregard for any intelligence and better insight. But imperceptibly the opponent falls into the hands of my defender, Didascalo. His arguments are staggering and at every turn enjoyably meant as a provocation of the taste of the time. In their joy of paradox and in their repeated reversal of my thoughts they correspond totally to the drawings they are meant to defend. He parries the accusation of hairsplitting as follows: *You yourself are the sophist, who wants to make rules for architecture that it has never known. What will you say when I prove to you that stringency, reason, and the imitation of the old hovels are incompatible with true architecture?*

Any rule, when raised to iron command, prunes the freedom of genius as well as the possibilities of development and the life of art in general. It's much more important, says my defender, to carry through the free power of invention against a falsely understood and narrow-minded trust in reason. At the end of my dialogue I spring again out of my role-playing and attack Mariette once more directly. His much labored and feminine *belle et noble simplicité,* that unspeakable fad of Winckelmann, is forced by me into the inescapable alternative that art either refrains from all variations and changes or atrophies in mere artsy-craftsy copies of empty rules. I was sure of having forged ahead far beyond sheer polemicism and the justification of Roman architecture to a scientific explanation of my own work.

It was an inexcusable mistake to react to the accusations of a critic. The only valid form of reaction is a new work. All else avails nothing. *Semper aliquid haeret.* Something is always left hanging. But this confrontation cost me more strength in regard to my health and more irretrievable time than it was worth.

From those dark days only a single bright spot remained in my memory: Cardinal Rezzonico, the nephew of the pope and the grand master of the Order of the Knights of Malta, commissioned me—possibly only from a whim and without ahead of time having come to terms thoroughly with my genius—with the renovation of the Church of S. Maria del Priorato on the Aventine and with the redesign of the Piazza dei Cavalieri di Malta. Of course, that was not the great building commission that I might have been entitled to, but it was a beginning anyway. It was my task to secure and to restore the deteriorated church. The chapel, consisting of a nave with each of four shallow side niches and a hardly projecting transept, had to remain untouched by the renovation. That reduced my spatial fantasies enormously, of course. After all, the grounds steeply sloping to the Tiber denied me daring designs. And once again the builder made the excuse about his presumably too-meager financial means. So I had to resort completely to my wealth of ideas on a small scale and had to be content with the securing of the foundation and the walls. I necessarily had to leave the structure itself untouched. If architecture is forced, I told myself, to preserve the power of human

creativity only in its narrowest criterion, then ornament must step
up to represent the naturelike dignity and majesty of a building. I
modified my Lateran project, which had veered into the visionary,
for the design of the chancel and submitted to scaling down. Thus
the framing position of columns and the arched semicircle of the
apse fall into one; I moved the altar forward to the crossing and
turned over much of the arrangement of details to the stucco
sculptor Tomasso Righi. The still life of the sarcophagus made a
place of death and memorial of the altar: the Place of Skulls as the
ground of rebirth. Anyway, it was the grave burial church of the
Roman Order of the Knights of Malta, and I felt the responsibility of responding to the appearance and the international standing of the Cavalieri di Malta, who had impressed me deeply even
in my childhood at processions and parades with their broad
mantels and their eight-pointed Maltese cross. These gentlemen
had always been for me the epitome of knighthood, the dignity
and the sacred purpose of charitable love for your fellow man. I
had found a row of tombs inside the church. They were now distributed symmetrically in the shallow niches of the nave and
made a part of my thematic program through a fantastic decoration that points to the omnipresence of death and fame in ever
new symbols. Taken all in all, it was a much too modest commission: far beneath my standard. Yet I was to succeed in forcing the
most extreme tensions into harmony in the smallest space, making a rule of irregularity, and raising all defined relationships of
size to the prerequisite of the effect on the viewer. Only by stepping out in front of the church door did the chance and the problem arise to meet the significance of the commission through the
uniqueness of the solutions. In front of the entrance to the gardens I put a flat-stretched gateway construction whose Palladian
succession of pilasters and false niches is at once parodied: The

pilasters, dispersed into frames jutting forward and back, into which bulky supports cut in under the molding, divide neither the structure nor forcefully mark the center part, whose triangular pediment is placed almost absurdly over the two inner supports that are inset too far. Most emblems, which allude to the military and maritime power of the Order of the Knights of Malta, meet the visitor in multiple variations.

I couldn't help crossing again and again the paths of the detestable Winckelmann, and so I asked friends whom I could trust implicitly to research the life of that repulsive upstart.

Even in school his Greek is said to have been better than his Latin. Presumably that is the source of his aversion to all things Roman. He despised that Rome which I loved so much, called it a bad copy of Greece, and considered our art to be derivative. And yet he lived in the Eternal City like in clover, had Angelica Kauffmann paint his portrait, and showed off with his Meissen service: a half dozen coffee cups without handles, a half dozen *cioccolata* cups with handles, plates and teapots, and other fancy pieces. In the cold season he resided in his comfortable rooms in the Palazzo Albani in the center of Rome; after Easter he accompanied his cardinal to Nettuno; he spent the summer months in the Castel Gandolfo, and couldn't get enough of money and luxury. Still, he remained that *homo vagus et inconstans,* as his matriculation booklet had certainly revealed him to be: an aimless and capricious fellow, who in all seriousness asserted in his writings that private parts had their special beauty:

Among testicles, the left is always larger, as it is found in nature, just as one has observed that the left eye sees more distinctly than the right.

And that under the title of *History of the Art of Antiquity*!

His whole hypocritical philhellenism circled around young Spartans, who appeared naked before the *ephori,* who did their

physical exercises naked, who were occupied exclusively with the
beauty of their naked bodies. Winckelmann's Greece is a naked
delusion. This German enthusiast had no inkling of history. He
saw Greece as a lost Eden and charged the Romans with being
second-class. The Hellenic *Laocöon,* of which he had become enamored, is in large part the work of the Roman restorer Agostino
Cornacchini. But the German never admitted any such thing. He
wanted nothing more than to lust after the naked bodies of
youths.

Still, in Germany, where a person is usually swallowed up by a
scholar or a critic, this sordid, miserable wretch had cosied up to
papal nuncio Alberigo Archinto, who was plagued by gout, who
in turn had recommended him to his friend, the Cardinal
Passionei, because the latter had urgent need of a librarian for his
collection of three hundred thousand stolen books. The *cazzone*
Winckelmann recognized his chance—he turned coat and con-
verted to Catholicism as though it were no more than a cattle
trade. If before, as a village schoolmaster, he had griped about
night sweats, insomnia, fainting, and a weak stomach, now he
blossomed at once, after he had abjured the *errores Lutheranae sec-
tae.* But as soon as he was about to make the sign of the cross with
his right hand, his left hand twitched, and on Ash Wednesday
when he was to be marked with ashes, his head made such con-
vulsive movements that the consecrated dirt was almost smeared
in his mouth. He sold his books in order to buy a fur coat, because
it was supposedly so cold in the libraries. Like a snake shedding
its skin, as a later biographer had to admit, the *cazzo* Winckelmann
gained a new wardrobe for himself every time he had gotten to
another rung on the ladder of his career. Sometimes he went
dressed as an uncloistered cleric in black silk cassock with blue,

yellow-edged collar and dark velvet trousers, although he had never been ordained, and then again he was seen in a coffee-brown *drap-d'Abbéville* coat with gold braid and a travel costume of English flannel. Always the *bella figura,* always that absolutely theatrical obscenity, and always his pockets filled with letters of recommendation. He had not been in Rome for very long, he had just begun his damage to Roman earth, when he had already rented a room in the Palazzo Zuccari, near the present Hotel Hassler beside the Trinità dei Monti. I was living around the corner on the Via Sistina, Goldoni nearby on the Via dei Condotti. Hardly had the German moved into his four-room apartment on the top floor of the Palazzo Albani, the present Palazzo del Drago on the Via Quattro Fontane on the Quirinal, than he bought himself a straw hat and—as a sign of his new rank as a private secretary, companion, and librarian of Cardinal Alessandro Albani—had it trimmed with violet silk. The German Winckelmann knew how you attained success quickly in Rome.

Anyone who wants to make his fortune in Rome, Casanova remarked, *must be a chameleon that is able to adapt to all the colors that light falls upon in his vicinity. He must be adroit and obliging, over sanctimonious, inscrutable, and flattering. He must be able to be nasty and still make an honorable impression. He must pretend to know less than he actually knows and always speak in one and the same tone of voice. He must practice patience and control the expression on his face and seem to be ice cold when another in his place would be all enthusiasm.*

Only now do I know and have comprehended that the Rome I idolized was so ailing that even the barbarians would have been able to destroy it. It is ridiculous to discuss Rome. It's as though one wanted to jam the universe between the two covers of a book. This Rome was really nothing more than a single gigantic sewer of intrigue and slander, just as all the academies and universities to this day are nothing but old boys' clubs and sewers of intrigue and slander because they are dominated either by senile old men or by ambitious men lusting for power who can do nothing but constantly plot and slander. Virgil had called upon the Romans to lead peoples as gentlemen. But these days an atmosphere of clerics and critics pollutes the city. If someone asks me where the best theater in the world can be seen, I always say: "Rome." All Rome is a theater. If you want a theater, then pick all of Rome; if you want a stage setting, then pick all of Rome. No director can stage it, no actor can play it, no stage designer can build it as the Romans do. Rome as a whole is the best and greatest theater in the world. There's nothing like it anywhere else. All of Rome is nothing more than a gigantic provincial-tragicomic-slapstick-theatrical monster. Rome is a punishment by God. And Rome is an international traffic junction. Today Rome has degenerated into the status of the capital of the Italians and fallen victim to building speculators. It is rotting like the papacy; it's nothing more than a tattered glorious rug that would fall apart as soon as it was dusted. That's why I hate and despise it so, and that's why I love and respect and admire it so immeasurably. Rome is not only the greatest art mill but at the same time the greatest institution for the destruction of art. Only in Rome can you really learn to despise human beings. According to legend Rome was founded by Romulus and Remus. Rhea Silvia had borne twin boys to Mars, the god of war. The children were cast into the Tiber and were washed ashore by a flood, where they were suckled by the Capitoline she-wolf. The shepherd Faustulus found the children and raised them. Afterward, through auspices, Romulus was given precedence over Remus, and so Romulus built the city of

Rome on the Palatine. He slew his brother when the latter jumped over the newly built city wall in mockery. This legend can be read as a simile of me and Winckelmann. From the beginning our path is determined by the god of war, from the beginning it is certain that there could only be war between us. As a symbol of Rome the Capitoline wolf nurtured and suckled Winckelmann as well as me. We were raised in the spirit of Faustulus, in which Winckelmann in Teutonic arrogance may recognize that Faustian urge for knowledge to which the Germans to this day appeal with stupendous narrow-mindedness. But mind you, it wasn't Faust but only a Faustulus. However that may be, the auspices recognized my prerogative as the sole legitimate successor of Romulus. Romulus became an architect, just as I was destined to become an architect from the beginning. But Remus-Winckelmann made fun of the wall built by Romulus, mocked it, and jumped over it in the direction of Greece and therefore had to die.

The meanest people in the world live in Rome. It is characteristic of a fallen society that it can enjoy only the raciness of frivolous corruption, as Winckelmann demonstrated. To tickle dulled sensations such an era requires what is most unheard-of, what is most disparate and repulsive, including sheer apathy that it can extol in triumph as the highest art. The general stultification of minds grazes on that inartistic apathy because it becomes, as it were, the ideal of their negative conditions. Only the mixture of blood, sperm, and holy water is taken for art, only what is shrill has a chance at all of being noticed. And I was and am the one who has to suffer most of all from it. So occasionally I get a bit mean.

The older I become, the more I respect malice, which I was actually forced by my enemies and murderers to respect properly. When someone practices such a thing as long as I was forced to practice it, he becomes better and better at it. That would not be true for a violinist, because his arm becomes more tired the more he practices. Not so with someone who etches with a cold needle. Because actually he doesn't etch with the cold needle but with his head. I make my etchings with it for the seam of my protective mantle, since otherwise I would freeze to death in this worldwide, eternal Roman winter.

Even the paths out of Purgatory lead to Rome. I know an address there: on Lungotevere Prati 12, a few steps from the Castel Sant'Angelo. The Church of Sacre Cuore del Suffragio. There in a side section lies the Museo delle Animi in Purgatorio, where in the showcases the remains of poor souls from Purgatory are preserved: fingerprints and handprints, black-charred traces of fire on paper and wood. The prints of three fingers of Maria Zaganti from Rimini or the nun Klara Scholers from the Westphalian Warendorf, presumably the daughter of a horse-trader con man. On a linen strip of her death shroud she left behind a burn mark that sent her religious sisters in the home convent Vinnenberg into a turmoil. I see her hysterical pious sisters directly before me when they report the event to the Holy See and convey the garment to Rome. Genuine discernible signs of the return of the deceased. And again and again branded messages from souls repenting in Purgatory. Abbot Panzani from Mantova left behind four wooden tablets with fiery traces of his hands, Josef Schlitz from Stralbe, with a print of five fingers, exhorted his brother Georg to hold a mass for the dead finally, and Luisa Le Senèchal, née Chauviers, pinched her sleeping husband in order to make him remember her: The burned marks on his nightcap are clear proof. Naturally, clerics made capital with all of that. Those from the Albani clan foremost.

I, too, from time to time was in the service of big-assed Albani, who had set his mind on a villa: one of the largest building projects in Rome. The cardinal was possessed by the idea of creating a living museum and had therefore ordered the restoration of every sculpture that could by any means be repaired. The restoration of the relief *Woman with Mirror* fell upon me, a work far beneath my capabilities, with which I admit I succeeded brilliantly. Even my arch enemy had to admit that. The Villa Albani flourished, later became the Villa Torlonia and finally the Villa of Il Duce Mussolini. So short is the path of history.

Again and again I read up on Livy and trained my imagination by him. After all, Livy's words had shown Hannibal the way across the Alps. On the history-soaked ground of the Aventine I was able to make clear my favorite idea of letting ancient Rome be glimpsed everywhere through the physiognomy of the modern city. In addition, the deliberate mixture of motif images of antiquity and the Baroque had the hidden task of screening the narrowness of the church and its square. But through the indestructible power of imagination the central guiding thought remained the restoration of what was lost in the past.

Oh, if only they had just one time let me build in a grand way!

The work proceeded sluggishly while I began my first plans for the décor in the Quirinal and Capitol palaces, as well as for Castel Gandolfo. Two years after the exhausting controversy with the miserable French critic, I was appointed by Clement XII as a *Cavaliere degli Speroni d'Oro*. But I presented to the cardinals a glorious series of presentation drawings of all my plans for the reconstruction for of S. Giovanni in Laterano.

Medals and honors are bills of exchange drawn on public opinion; their value depends on the credit of the issuer. Blinded by the highest favor, I was taken in anew by pompous asses and loudmouths, who in splendid robes strolled on holy ground, and starry-eyed as a child and contrary to my better judgment, I believed that from now on everything would improve.

My plan aimed again at overpowering the observer: Since the vault of the cupola again reached far above the ceiling of the bay, by gazing through the lower and darker bay the impression had to arise of looking into a light-flooded, completely irreal rotunda. And this illusory effect was to be emphasized by indirect lighting that from a large round window in the easterly front wall and from hidden apse windows focused the brightness at the structure of the altar and on the silhouette of the positioned columns. I meant to transform the choir and the apse into a stage for a Christian mystery play, to perfect the contrast of brightness and shadow by a totally un-Roman illumination from hidden sources of light, borne by the basic idea of treating the church not as a uniformly planned and structured space but to set the choir as a view and scenic image opposing the spectator's space of the nave.

I saw myself already building, saw myself leaving the dungeon world of merely thought-of and drawn architecture that had become too cramped—but again nothing was to come of it.

And why?

Because my ideas of grandeur would have exhausted all available monies for the reconstruction. Again and again my plans became ignominious because of so-called reality. Bent backs and smooth words: That was all.

The wind of misfortune again began to blow.

The Curia screamed in horror at my plan to transform the Lateran into an opera house. As tragic as this was also for me, these ordained gentlemen with their secret prostate ailments, cackling all over the place like startled chickens, outrageously gesticulating, slavering sacrilege and worse, had something really touchingly ridiculous about them. I still see them before me clasping their hands in horror above their heads, moaning at my explanations, struggling for words between uncontrolled rage and speechless bewilderment to refute me, and how they finally unceremoniously put me out the door. One of the breviary-panting clerics even insisted on having me led to the Inquisition by the Swiss Guards wearing costumes designed by Michelangelo, while another contented himself with the penance of a mercifully short Rosary in honor of the Madonna.

As crushed as I was, I couldn't help leaving the Vatican, that sepulcher of mummies and vice-deities, with a diabolical grin and letting my laughter echo in the colonnades in front of the Church of St. Peter. The whole clerical bunch—nothing but parrots. The Vatican— a mindless place, inhabited by mindless men, kept alive for centuries by mindless men. The Vatican believes that the world would end if it itself ended. Only mindless men believe that about themselves. Someone once told the complete truth when he said that the Catholic Church has the destruction of humanity on its conscience, humanity in a state of chaos, in the final analysis thoroughly unfortunate humanity. "Millions and even billions are indebted to the Catholic Church," the tinkerer of the wheel of history and brother in spirit remarks with absolute correctness, "for their having been destroyed and ruined completely." If I were religious, then I would be a Cartharist. The Catharists, who were completely wiped out, believed that Creation was not the work of God but of the Devil. Let all the clerics make the sign of the cross over me, I alone blessed myself. Our lot is indebted to no one, but everyone is indebted to us for everything. And like the critics, the clerics practice their spiritual indecencies incessantly.

Of course, my short amusement had a high price. More than ever before I sought shelter in my fantasy, in a preciously guarded inner holy place where I could escape the adversity of the outer world and draw what my voices showed me.

There are moments in life in which the question becomes essential about whether you can think differently from the way you think and see differently from the way you see, insofar as you want to see and think further. Anyway, I made thought, with its necessary clarity, a principle.

Nothing in architecture can assume shape, I made it clear to the Holy Office, that is not thought and felt and in figuratively spatial forms foreseen in the imagination of the architect. So the architectonic design begins with seeing, I said, that is, with the ability to apprehend and experience the world about us in the shapes of images and spaces. But construction and design are inseparably bound to one another. Those were words for deaf ears. Just talking to the wind. Shape is the goal of architectonic design. Architectonic design, I said, is the ability to give your objective a spatial shape: It is a seeking, resourceful contact with material and space; it is the imaginative play with light and the muses of beauty, of proportion, and rhythm, the harmony of forms and their suspenseful order. Design, I told the spiritual dignitaries and well-heeled merchants of the Holy Office, is the unflagging struggle for the expression of semblance, for only someone who understands how to master forms can design. That's what I told them—and they threw me out. Where are those dignitaries headed with their dignity?

I felt like a broken yardstick. I had successes—and that sounds like scorn—only with sketches of fireplace and interior decoration with the design of the *Caffè degl'Inglesi* in the Egyptian style.

The whole world fears time, but time fears the pyramids. When in the palace I was a throne watcher and a sandal bearer; King Merenre appointed me prince and governor of Upper Egypt, from Elephantine to Middle Egypt, although that post had never been delegated to a servant before. His Majesty sent me then to Abhat to get a life chest along with its lid, as well as an expensive, marvelous top for the pyramid "Merenre's beauty gleams." His Majesty then sent me to Elephantine to bring a false door of granite with its sacrificial slab as well as gate blocks of granite and door frames of granite and sacrificial slabs of the upper chamber of the mistress "Merenre's beauty gleams." I traveled downstream with them to "Merenre's beauty gleams" on six escort ships, three cargo ships, three trailing ships, and a single ship of soldiers. Never at the time of any king were Abhat and Elephantine reached by only a single ship of soldiers. His Majesty sent me to Hatnub to bring a large sacrificial slab from the crags. In seventeen days I managed to get the sacrificial slabs down, which were quarried in Hatnub. I had them taken downstream on a convoy ship. Although there was no water in the canals, I landed safely at "Merenre's beauty gleams." Furthermore His Majesty sent me out to dig five canals in Upper Egypt, in order to be able to get further granite for the pyramids. I did what the court wished. The whole world fears time, but time fears the pyramids.

I had sunken to the level of a restorer and decorator—but I had to live. Therefore, with gnashing teeth I consented.

Instead of the reconstruction of the Lateran I had to concern myself with fireplaces, console tables, wall coverings, clock cases, commodes, chandeliers, stuffed chairs, candelabra, and sedans and to increase my meager honorarium through collections and trade in antiquities, mostly with snobbish English customers like the earl of Exeter. The earl of Carlisle even demanded from me the production of a resplendent carriage like the one he had discovered on my *Vedute di Roma.* I had fallen, as you would say today, to the rank of a fashionable designer for those Englishmen who roamed also through Rome on their Grand Tour. My fireplace frameworks went to Holland to a wealthy merchant named

John Hope, as a marriage dowry to the salon and library of Gorhambury House, to Wedderburn Castle in Berwickshire as well as to Wardow Castle in Hampshire to Lord Arundell. Among my customers was also the family of Cardinal Rezzonico, for whose office rooms in the Quirinal Palace I also worked, as well as for the fittings of the offices of Senator Abbondio Rezzonico in the Senatorial Palace on the Capitol. Today these works, what a shame, are deposited in Minneapolis in thoroughly uncultured America. Heeding dictates by the very newest fashion the tables were borne by winged chimeras with goat's feet, and I mounted the silliest ornaments from favorite examples of Roman antiquity: with lions and sphinxes, feathered griffins and dragons, with Hermes pilasters and steles, with wall candelabra and garlands. It was to me as though I had ended up again in the theater workshop of a miserable provincial stage. Nothing but rubbish— whereas I would have given my life to be permitted finally to build.

In short order new etchings filled the empty cashbox: *Diverse maniere d'adornare i cammini ed ogni altra parte degli edifizi*. Wild mixtures emerged: Egyptian temple attendants, wingéd graces, weighed-down stone ashlars, soaring obelisks, chandeliers surrounded by flying mythological creatures, mummies as caryatids twined about by vegetative ornaments, gods with animal heads, slaves and scarabs, lions and alligators, as though I spoke the language of pharaoh-loving Egypt mania and its ridiculous embellishments. For example, I created an eagle with too-large claws and too-mighty a head and arranged the feathers of its outspread wings like the reed pipes of a shepherd's flute. I had become furious and disappointed, deeply offended, unhappy, and nasty to myself. My contemporaries were estranged and inimicable to my grotesque world. Only later generations would understand me. I was certain of that.

To the general dismay the interior decoration of the *Caffè degl'Inglesi* showed darkly towering horror architecture of showy façades with heavy ashlars through the openings of which the gaze could sweep far into the desert. The elegant coffee counter turned for me into the vestibule of a spurious shrine. Among the animal gods who rest on the molding, the grasshopper stands on equal basis with the crocodile.

And despite that I flattered myself, in my defiance and my hurt, in having liberated Egyptian as well as Etruscan architecture of that blemish that had been attached to them until now. In my designs I had succeeded in linking Greek style with the Egyptian and the Etruscan.

I had always objected to the dictum of critics that we had to strive for what is Greek in order to let ourselves be enslaved exclusively by it. I have also found beauty in other places where it has no Greek origin. No artist who wants to earn a name and respect can be satisfied with being only the copyist of a stylistic trend. Anyone who with clever deliberation links the Greek, Etruscan, and Egyptian with one another opens the path at the same time to new ornaments and new means of expression. I believe in the creative power of mergence and amalgamation. With increasing age, I turned my architectural drawings, which I finally knew I would never be allowed to build, more and more into sublime Nature paintings, into tattered rocky bottoms or ghostly caves of a landscape formed out of crumbling walls, collapsed vaults, and cracked projections of columns.

That's how my soul's landscape looked, too: ghostly, torn apart, debilitated, crumbled, burst. If we wanted and dared to create an architecture in accordance with the nature of our soul, says the philosopher, then the labyrinth would have to be our model. To the growing irritation of travelers who wished to orient themselves with my etchings, I increasingly gave more a *veduta ideata* in place of a *veduta esatta*. I had found for myself the balance between idea and perception, between dreamed infinity and realized outer world—but building had been eternally denied me.

In my last Roman years I once again tried a business collaboration with my son Francesco, with artist entrepreneurs such as Bartolomeo Cavaceppi and a young English sculptor named Joseph Nollekens. But the thing fell through. I could not collaborate with anyone. No one tolerated me, and likewise I tolerated no one. So I lived as a dealer of antiquities and a landscape artist, as an original and an outsider, in the end even as an attraction for those traveling to Rome, for my name had been bandied about as far as Scotland and Finland. And everyone, everyone who came, did not want to see my architectural plans but the eccentric, the screwball, the unsuccessful fantast who was a prisoner in his own prison visions. Already legends were curling around my person like ivy around a weather-beaten column. How much those lie, who presumably respect me.

The reproach of hubris threads through my biography. Again and again my contemporaries, in their narrow-mindedness, called out in warning to me that *non plus ultra* as it stands on the Columns of Hercules: Do not proceed further! And always this cry came from people who did not know the urge to recognize, violate, and cross over limits. I had to hear *Pride comes before the Fall,* and even more: *Pride is the Fall!* Icarus had come to experience that just as Bellerophon did, who soared into forbidden precincts on his winged horse Pegasus. I was called haughty and presumptuous while I was reflecting about why people again and again rebelled against borders set them. Borders separate and seem unmovable. People build their experiences on them. But it is not sufficient simply to bump against borders: You have to bump yourself against borders, for countries, epochs, and above all minds differentiate at borders. A border is not a thing where something stops, rather a border is where something begins. No artist can accept borders as given. Faits accomplis are a monstrosity for a creative human being. For me the border has always been the place of knowledge; but small minds didn't want to recognize that because they didn't even have the courage to follow me to the border. There the path did not end; there it first began. Something is recognized as a deficiency only when at the same time you have gone past it. And the more often someone strides past his borders, the more strongly he senses the shortcoming of not being able to extend himself still farther. Any border can be moved. But that in no way means to deny borders completely. Doesn't the border awaken the nostalgic idea that behind it lies something more beautiful, more grand? Doesn't the dignity of an artist consist specifically of his visions? Doesn't his pride come from that? This pride has nothing to do with self-love. But if he had that, then the artist would mistreat himself constantly with the brutal treads of his boots.

I agree much more with my countryman Pico della Mirandola, who once said: *A sacred pride should grip us of not being satisfied with the mediocre but to strive (for we can do it, if we want to) with the exertion of all our strength to attain the highest. Let us scorn what is of this earth, let us ignore what is of heaven, let us leave absolutely everything worldly behind us in order to hasten to the abode out of this world, in the proximity of the sublime deity. We do not need to think of stepping back, of being satisfied with second rank, let us strive for dignity and glory. To attain the highest.* That's what I wanted, too. But they didn't let me, they simply wouldn't let me.

Barely fifty years old, I had become an emotionally crushed, most deeply embittered and disappointed man to whom his life's dream had been persistently denied. I think you can see it in my depiction of the *Antichità di Tivoli:* The sheets become ever more fantastic, in ever larger format, with an ever richer nuanced cast of shadows—but I had become weary of detailed calculation and had lost my polemic ambition. I had become resigned. I countered the popular image of the noble creation of the human spirit with wild, bizarre trees, bushes, and creeping plants with their destructively proliferating force. Increasingly, elements of the irrational and ambiguous interested me. I etched on a hard surface and in doing so abandoned cross-hatching, since parallel lines sufficed for me, with which, however, I changed the direction of every detail. I covered the whole plate with those deliberately placed lines, with whose strength and intensity I shaped the intended tone values correspondingly without thus leaving out the brightest light. Only after this mode of work did I set the light with a varnish coat, which I applied with the brush, as one highlights a drawing with white. In this way the lights had a unheard-of daring; this freedom of execution substituted for the at times pettily forced precision of the ordinary copperplate etching. Only then did I start the nitric acid with a care and patience that no one would have credited to my hotheadedness—*Where patience is lacking, deeds appear to be misdeeds,* says the philosopher—covered the surfaces to be toned down one after the other, and repeated the procedure with certain plates again and again. Let's be deliberate, I said to myself, here I am making three thousand drawings at once. My goal was the complete control of a nuanced technique of etching in the finest detail.

But I was deeply depressed; it was my soul that was most deeply etched.

Only Nature, with its ever-returning cycle, affected me like balsam. But I let myself be deceived by this humbug because Nature is *femininum:* always with the tapping of sperm, with sexual congress, in mind. On my solitary forays through the Alban Hills I admired the formations of cliffs and cascades of water, the erratic boulders and glorious views of the palace and the Garden of Sallust: For me architecture was transformed back into Nature. There a temple encloses an almond tree, the towering walls and graceful shafts of columns in which the cliffs extend toward the sky—and all this only the natural soil for grasses and bushes. Valley and sky grow together over the thin line of the horizon as a distant film behind a towering stone massif. I restrained from drawing the famous grottoes. Let travelers use their own eyes and senses and no longer rely on illustrated guides. With my English, Scottish, and French friends, the few honest and faithful who had remained for me, I was drawn again and again to Tivoli to the snake-guarded halls and colonnades that dreamed of the plans of Hadrian to build a capacious summer palace that would collect on one spot and outdo the Stoa Poikile and the Academy of Athens, the tower of the misanthropist Timon, whom I understood better and better, the Canopus of Alexandria, the Zempe Valley in Thessaly—a wonder of the world beyond all world wonders. I took part in the excavations by Gavin Hamilton and gave my advice and support to the archaeologist.

Hadrian's great dream stirred the fire in me once more. The Villa Adriana was again a powerful challenge. And with the mellowness of one growing old, who had lost all illusions, I knew that I would have been the only one who could build the villa in accordance with the emperor's visions. My landscapes came into being during the seventies, accompanied by a series of unetched drawings under the impression of the savage wilderness into which the expansive fields of ruins were banished for centuries. I added few commentaries to the landscapes of the Villa Adriana. But instead I provided an appropriate picturesque effect and experimented with a multitude of limned positions in which the linear outline of objects dissolved flickering or in dull two-dimensionality. It was no longer a matter for me of providing so many theatrical effects. Also, the figures distributed over the rubble are transported from the present in a curious way. They either seem to gesticulate and to spout off like buffoons and pantomimists in the spirit of the commedia dell'arte, like actors from a piece by Goldoni, or you could believe they were fellahs with large lances. A society of dwarfs inhabits a city built for giants. But they are never merely figures to illustrate scale. Like scorpions and vipers at this unreal place of oblivion, these deformed, hunchbacked lemurs that now sun their twisted limbs on the ruins of the wall, now with agitated gestures point at details of the architecture, are all divested of the attributes of daily life and squat with spidery arms in the light of this palace lying in the sleep of death.

Through the reworking of my old plates I brought the views more and more in line with one another. Only the shadows became longer and more profound, for now the transition of art into Nature became my theme. I summed up my reflections in my last depiction of the Colosseum. It shows the monstrous round crater of the amphitheater—not least also as the symbol of the arena of my senseless life—from an imaginary bird's-eye view. The truth and power of my effects, the correct cast and clarity of my shadows, indeed, even the representation of the tone values, were

based on precise observation day by day. I studied my surroundings under full sunlight as well as by the light of the moon, in
which the masses of the architecture appear so tremendous and
possess a stability, charm, and harmony that frequently trail far
behind the effect of the flickering illumination by day. Since I observed in detail the light effects from nearby as well as from the
distance and at all hours of the day, at the same time I memorized
them. Doing so, I renounced the pathos of resistance, transformed the world wonder into a spectacle of Nature, and gave it
the melancholy seclusion of an extinguished volcano. I saw it as a
colossal skeleton from distant heroic ages and thought of Dante's
Circle of Hell.

My works were always a direct reflection of my inner life. So I
don't have to illustrate to you separately by way of this example
how it was. The death of my patron Clement XIII forced me into
manifold and hectic activity in enervating everyday work. All my
plans had to be postponed for financial reasons. But it wasn't only
the lack of money that made me stagnate. I had become unspeak-
ably weary, and I felt leaden, empty, used up, burned out. Ever
more painfully did I become aware of my growing old, and my
body began to play its underhanded tricks on me more and more.
For long enough I had not understood how, in my life gone
wrong, something as serious as aging could strike me.

Then from Pompeii came tremendously fresh news of wondrous excavations, and I remembered my trip to Naples, which I
had taken in my young years. Pompeii always exerted a great attraction to me—after all, the excavations also promised archaeological discoveries that were quick to turn into cash. Admittedly,
the entire sojourn there was soon soured because of that unspeakable Winckelmann, who likewise was looking around at the same

place and believed he had to comment on everything in his forced clever girlish way. This time my son Francesco accompanied me—the most talented among the good-for-nothings who had crawled from the womb of my insatiable wife—to the excavations near Vesuvius, and for the first time we worked hand in hand.

My son: the sad remains from the fragments of my family. My drawings just wouldn't come out right. I abstained from any theatrical gesture and suggestive exaggeration, with a coarsely cut reed pen indicated only the outlines of columns, walls, and temple fronts and crosshatched irregularly in a dirty brown ink to emphasize the hard contours. Some few figures, workers at the excavation or bewildered tourists, are mostly ornamental details. No more dramatization of simple ruins of walls into cyclopean structures. I constantly felt as though I were looking over the shoulder of that revolting German. That crippled me.

I remembered how once at a social gathering I had heard him babble about his climb of Vesuvius: It couldn't be denied that a foretaste of Hell was connected with the climb of such a fiery mountain, if you didn't want to approach it preferably like the ancients as a workshop of the smith of the gods. Frightful the lack of any kind of vegetation. Slag everywhere, and more slag. The terrible work of the primal blacksmith and his apprentices. *We climbed upward to the edge of Hell, we even stepped into its realm, where the glowing streams of lava glowed next to us in slowly crackling progress. Around us glowing chunks hailed down; they bounced about like little demons. We had become drenched while climbing. Then we dried our clothes at the hellish stream of lava. And Winckelmann, who stands before you, unclad as an ancient statue, roasted doves at the fiery river of the volcano.* How I loathed that German, how he revolted me, how I hated him.

On my last journey into the South in the year 1777—the so-called Werther fever was rampant in Europe—I was already a man fatally ill. I felt like a boat on a desolate ocean, pushing the empty horizon ahead of me. Together with my only modestly talented son Francesco—one's own child is always the most reckless and disappointing—I wanted to survey and draw the Doric temples of the Greek colony of Poseidonia on the Gulf of Salerno. My way led through a malaria-ridden region. The destination was Paestum, and the wind of misfortune blew about me anew.

The ubiquitously mincing *cazzone* Winckelmann had naturally likewise made his appearance at the place, delivered his commentary, and had had to call the temples the most astonishing and fair that he had ever encountered. He could leave nothing uncommented upon. Like a critic he also could not resist using his ink on the devastation and furtive abolition of independent thought. His thoughtless ideas brought to paper were nothing more than the tracks of a limping man on the sand, and his understanding of art resembled that of a woman who is bedecked with gold and jewels but who wears a tattered gown. The *stronzetto* Winckelmann never understood what a work of art imparts: It is not its own tangible self but that which lies outside of it and cannot be grasped by hands but rather only by the imagination. The German always made a dreadful fuss about his theory. Noise is always the most impertinent of all interruptions because it breaks, it smashes

thoughts. Winckelmann did not study in order to attain knowledge and insight but to be able to babble and gain a respectability
for himself. He did not aim at insight but at a patron. He always
had to fill the holes in his mediocre realizations with empty
phrases. That's what makes his writing so boring on the one hand
and so influential on the other. His science was a means to him,
not an end. Therefore his mind resembled a gut that sorts out all
foods undigested. The very foundation, says the philosopher, on
which all our knowledge and science rests is what is inexplicable.
Winckelmann, on the contrary, always wanted to explain and derive everything because he constantly had his personal need and
advantage in mind. He could never admit that artworks of all ages
could exist side by side peacefully. He made rapacious animals out
of them that tear one another to pieces and accord dominance
only to what is Greek.

The reason for that — is Winckelmann's thoroughly polemical nature, that Teutonic *bellum omnium contra omnes*. Artists and observers of art are fellow wanderers. If they want to arrive together, they have to start out together. But Herr Winckelmann always had to be the one in front of everybody and the first one there. Knowledge and insight cannot, as critics believe, be enriched by so-called discussion and comparison but only by independent observation. Winckelmann always wanted to compare and demonstrate. But art is not a problem in arithmetic. Its equation never works out exactly. Great shrewdness, which one must grant the *cazzone,* may well qualify for a career but it doesn't make an artist. His false doctrine, taken from a false viewpoint and sprung from a bad intention, will be valid only for a limited time. An original thought was always alien to Winckelmann because he could support himself only with examples and with what he had learned. He relied on concepts of his supposedly analytical judgment and tried to transmit these through visual perception. That had to fail because he himself was not at all capable of vital perception because of his ridiculous thought processes. In the present intellectually impotent period, distinguished by the respect of what was bad in every genre, this cream puffery was bound to be very succcessful. And as far as this so-called philhellenism is concerned, I can say only that the eye will become dulled by staring too long at an object and will see nothing more. Likewise, reason becomes inefficient and confused by continued thought in one direction. Winckelmann stared constantly at Greek things and thought constantly only in that direction. The German peacock lacked two decisive abilities: to judge and to have original thoughts. From this came his lifelong attempt to set a crown on a dwarf. While Winckelmann, with his supposed appetite for observation, had looked steadily only in his books, I had always looked into the world and recognized that the world is not only flawed but misguided. The highest maxim of the German was to get by with the least application of thought, because for him thought was nothing but a burdensome hardship. In the case of Winckelmann, in whose mind a world as idea never found a place, the intellect as a tool in the service of career became a slave of necessity. From this comes also the limitation of his barbaric and undignified conversations. Winckelmann saw me, like a critic, as a hunter sees the hare that can be enjoyed and be dressed only after its death, and which one therefore must simply shoot at as long as one lives. This washed-up preacher's toady is the best proof that stupidity is the mother of the race of humankind: *Humani generis mater nutrixque profecto stultitia est.*

Talent labored for money and fame. It gleamed only in the hidden light of the Greeks: a shooting star at which everyone in the world ohs and ahs. On the other hand, I am a fixed star. It stands fixed in the firmament, has its own light, doesn't belong to one system or another but to the world, its appearance not changed by the change of a point of view. But just because of its height its light requires many years before it becomes visible to the dull earth dweller. First of all, at its appearance what is bad stands in the way of what is great. The ill fate of its merits is that they must wait until they are recognized. On the other hand, Winckelmann

could not distinguish gold from copper because he revered anything that gleamed. His fame rests on the lamentable lack of
judgmental power of the critics. Having once come into credit, his
deceptions defied whole centuries. His supporters in turn praised
him only because all the world praised him. They wanted to exalt
themselves through splendor and not to come too late with their
tribute. If Winckelmann lived on borrowed glory, his supporters
lived on doubly borrowed glory. Winckelmann is nothing more
than a Herostratos, who, because he had no better idea, burned
down a temple to become famous.

The impudently cooked-up fame of Winckelmann's asshole
erudition came into being through unfair praise, bribed critics,
and clerical might. The German succeeded in leading all the elegant world on a leash, for anyone who writes for fools always find
a large public that confuses the purchase of writings with the ac-
quisition of their contents. This fame resembles the bladder of an
ox by which you float something that would naturally sink. The
barbarians are already there; the Vandals can't be far behind. This
bestia trionfante was always surrounded by a chorus of bootlickers.
Like liquid manure this fame poured down on everyone, supported by the paid claques of academies, universities, and
gazettes. No, Winckelmann did not stand above his century. He
was and remains a favorite of the masses, the pack, the alleyways
and anterooms. Recognition and respect are dependent on distance, not on the gossip of an applauding mob that constantly
fawns on someone. Winckelmann never understood that, for he
never thought for himself. His century was also mine. To the
short span of time in which they live, great minds are like grand
buildings to a small square on which they stand, says the philosopher. You don't see them because you stand too close to them. But

when a century lies between them, they are recognized. You can think through only what you know. But since the *stronzo* Winckelmann knew nothing about architecture, he could also not think it through. The German peacock could not think for himself but was a parrot with the blind ambition of becoming a European songbird. His erudition was only an expression of his insipidity. However often people are there who babble about Greek culture, they are seldom those who think. For this German sycophant, reading was just a surrogate for thinking. You should read only when your own fountain of thought runs dry. Winckelmann read too much, as is the bad habit of all ivory tower scholars. He literally read himself stupid, for during reading the mind of an excerpter and self-showman is the hotbed of strange ideas. Winckelmann was nothing more than a insatiable glutton of paper.

Goethe to Eckermann on February 16, 1827: *You learn nothing when you read it, but you become something.* The original thinker becomes acquainted with authorities regarding his opinion only in retrospect, whereas someone like Winckelmann starts with authorities. Merely acquired knowledge stuck to him like a fake nose. The professional scholar is to an original thinker like a research historian to an eyewitness: The latter speaks only from a direct perception of the matter, whereas the professional scholar reports what this one has said and that one has opined and someone else has objected to. The original thinker is like a prince: He is direct and acknowledges no one over himself. But the blind adherent resembles the rabble in the lanes that needs rules to follow. Anyone who thinks for himself is an original thinker. Someone who thinks for others is just looking for applause. The thought of the original thinker walks its own path like a tomcat. Applause, however, is nothing more than the final act of destruction, for it rattles down like hell fire. Winckelmann was by nature envious of me, plagued by the insignificance of his thought. Envy, the philosopher says, is the soul of the bond of all mediocrity that, having silently come together by chance, flourishes everywhere and is opposed to honored individuals. There are two ways to handle merit: Either have some yourself or allow none to be valid. As soon as a talent stirs anywhere, all the mediocre people of that field try unanimously to hide it and hinder it in every possible way from becoming known. In a unique way this Winckelmann, too, fell victim to envy, for a method used frequently by envy for disparagement is the unscrupulous praise of what is terrible. Since critics did not want to let me rise, they praised noble simplicity and quiet grandeur. Of course, as soon as what is terrible has validity, what is good is lost.

In order to demonstrate how senseless Winckelmann's assertions are, I partially made his demands literally my own—in order to arrive at completely different, that is to say, correct conclusions. His rule for the artist reads: *Imitation of antiquity.*

Paris, 1790: In the atelier of Jacques-Louis David several painters have banded together into a strange sect. They are dressed like ancient statues in a toga, converse in the Greek language, and every morning at five o'clock jump into the Seine to toughen themselves. They claim to model themselves in their art and their way of life after the example of ancient Greece in order to return the virtues of the Athens of yore to the new Republic. French revolutionary architecture, as a rule designed before the Revolution and oddly executed by Royalists, by no means forgoes the order of Greek columns. Absolutely everywhere there can be glimpsed the Abbot Marc-Antoine Laugier's theory of the primeval hut, as he placed it at the beginning of his *Essai sur l'architecture* in the second edition of 1755. And this primeval hut, supposedly the original structure of all architecture, reveals again a surprising similarity to Greek temples.

Vienna, 1890: The Ringstrasse was recently completed. It is the triumph of historicism. Painters and architects burrowed in the past like opera directors in the prop department. Even Parliament itself was built in the classic Greek style.

At Bergstrasse 19 there lives a Jew who, in his study full of antique art objects, for the purchase of which he spends a great part of his savings, proposes a remarkable theory. He compares the memories of humankind with a city in ruins. In order to explain psychological disorders, he falls back on Oedipus and the figures of Greek mythology. In 1904 he himself suffers a curious partial amnesia on the Acropolis. The archaic visions of the Ringstrasse architecture are not without influence on his ideas of emotional life, for those architects researched cultural forms of the past like archaeologists and uncovered the remains of one or another epoch in order to use them for the requirements of the moment.

Likewise in Vienna, in a less elegant quarter not far from the West Terminal, at Stumpergasse 29, a young man named Adolf Hitler has lived since 1907. He wants to become an artist but fails to be admitted to the Academy. He lives miserably from the sale of his drawings and watercolors, on which he repeatedly depicts the splendid buildings on the Ringstrasse. Some years later he will gather a series of other failed artists about him in order with them to plunge the world into calamity.

Munich, 1906: the young Giorgio de Chirico arrives in the Bavarian capital, called *the New Athens*. Leo von Klenze and Friedrich von Gärtner have rebuilt it in the Neoclassic style.

Arcades, columns, and open, columned porticoes determine the cityscape. In de Chirico they awaken the longing for Thessaly, the land of his origin. In 1920 the painter writes on his pictures: *Pictor classicus sum* and presents himself in the form of an ancient marble bust.

Munich, 1937: The House of German Art, erected by Paul Ludwig Troost in Doric style, is dedicated. On the street Bavarian daughters file past in Greek tunics; they carry the oversize statues of Pallas Athena. According to Hitler, you see, the Teutons are the natural descendants of the Doric peoples, and German culture must claim the Greek heritage for itself. So architecture and sculpture of the Third Reich become early Greek. *For it is only a reversion,* as Goebbels emphasizes. Predominant is the idea of *eternal return,* of *regressive backward steps* of which Freud speaks, that fascination for antiquity, or more exactly, Classical Greece, which is perceived not only in the sense of Winckelmann as a natural origin but is laid claim to exclusively. It is the Winckelmannian longing for the *pure radiance of the past.*

Antiquity had to be dead for a Renaissance to come into being. All renaissances henceforth were to stand under the sign of nostalgia for a lost whole and sensitivity. Art and architecture had the task of thinking of the whole and giving it expression. That pertains as much to French classicism as it does to Hölderlin and Nietzsche and all those latecomers who set out to seek the land of the Greeks with their souls.

In Rome, in a small studio on the Tiber, not far from the Ponte Sant'Angelo, lived a man who called himself Alceo Dossena and who could demonstrate that he was the creator of a number of sculptures from various epochs, which had been acquired by a series of collections and museums for decades at high prices. These are works of classical antiquity, Romanticism, the Gothic period, the Renaissance, and the Baroque, in marble, terra-cotta, and wood. How many pieces are involved exactly, no one knows to this day. All that is known is that some of these works were extraordinary discoveries in the history of art, about which in the meanwhile extensive scientific literature exists. Then toward the end of 1928 the world of art was astonished by the report that all these works had been created by one man and also that desperate clinging to claims of authenticity was of no use. The incident was one of those unheard-of events and so unprecedented that word of it ran across the whole world through the press. No event had shaken the art world in such a way since the theft of the Mona Lisa. This man put everything in question that had tediously been developed in confidence regarding genuine art. Without a doubt the man was not a forger but an artist, if other reproductive experts such as Oistrach and Rostropovich are so designated: not creatively but re-creatively. Handicraft, the most natural thing in the world, is here transformed into a dimension of astonishment beyond expert. If this case was not to mean the bankruptcy of the theory of art, then Dossena's work had to be so good that the deception was justified. Then this unknown man from the Tiber had to be an unprecedented virtuoso who had more at his disposal than experts could suppose in a living man. In any case, art history knows no parallel to him. Dossena's pride is not clouded by vanity when he confesses: "Yes indeed, it was me, it is me. I created those many marveled and admired sculptures, all those sarcophagi, Madonnas with Child, angels, reliefs, all those things . . . And so from my hand came all the sculptures that truly deserve to become as treasured as the genuine Donatellos, Verocchios, Fiesoles . . ." As a nine-year-old child Alceo Dossena, the son of poor people from Cremona, had begun his career with a stonemason. He learned everything by hard work. He built violins that were as good as very good old violins. He learned every *kind of sculpting, was familiar as well with carving from wood. He prepared sketches for churches and those for modern apartment buildings with plans that contained every detail. This man never belonged to the world of art. He didn't count in society, he didn't exhibit. His skills came to be noticed by a few deceitful art dealers who exploited him and had him work for wages for almost a decade. The entire naïveté of this class of craftsmen characterizes a statement by Dossena: "I have even worried now and then whether people also get their money's worth with my works." Roughly, they took in millions. Dossena received orders from dealers for works in the style of this or that master. He then went to the provincial museums and immersed himself in a few works of that master. At home in many cases he made sketches of what he himself wanted to fashion, tore them up then, and began his work in his studio at once with the actual materials. It is difficult to imagine that a man could execute so many objectively good things without belonging to a "circle," without finding official recognition, also without being "unacknowledged" or feeling "unacknowledged." Additionally, there is his fanaticism regarding the material. From childhood on, his work as a stonemason in the repair of old churches and a preference for the structure of marble, made him study the stone very exactly in regard to the changes—in each instance according to its placement perhaps at the west portal, on the south side, or in the interior—to which it was exposed. He took pieces home with him, compared and examined them. Rome, the treasure chest for marble of any age, increased his passion, and probably from that arose his wish to create something ancient. So he became acquainted with the life of marble, and his inclination and his ability put him in the position of artfully toning down marble as the work to be created dictated. This toning or preparation was just as necessary for him as stylistic absorption in the style of an erstwhile master. In addition to these two goals*

of projecting himself into the temperament of old masters and into com-
plete adaptation of the material, the artistic mutilations and damages,
as far as they exist, lose their basic significance. For the man who from
childhood on lived with the old works in the condition in which he
found them, the damages must appear like something, such as the
patina, that immediately enhanced the optical and plastic charm.
Dossena says: "I was born in our time, however with the soul, the taste,
and the sensitivity of a different age." His technique exhibited the most
extreme academic care. Without any kind of sculptural or graphic
sketch, in a few minutes, and without haste, figures came into being in
high and bas-relief. With the same ease he modeled a head, and quite
suddenly there was the smile on the face of a woman to whom the
Greeks could have prayed two thousand years ago. All his works pro-
ceeded without affectation, thus without mystification. At times
Dossena also sang an opera melody, smiled his sour Gioconda smile,
and asserted that his name was Alceo Dossena—and not Giambattista
Piranesi.

The older the world becomes and the more the Greek past
fades away and its loss seems irretrievable, the greater the longing,
and soon also more uncannily its forms of expression grow.

It begins with the bloody festivals in honor of the Goddess of
Reason, which take place at the behest of Robespierre, and ends
with the processions of the Pan Athenians in the streets of
Munich, in front of the Propylaia of Klenze and the colonnades of
the last classicist Speer under the gaze of a corporal who philoso-
phizes fanatically: *Never was humanity closer to antiquity in its ap-*
pearance and its perception than today.

Winckelmann's dream of the revivification of the Greek past
was fulfilled. He made possible the Doric column next to the concentration camp. The masquerades in Greek style that were

mounted by the Nazis to celebrate the Day of German Art were the disguise of a desire to surpass, as it one day had sprung from the mind of a postcard architect when he happened upon the façades of the Ringstrasse.

Thought logically to the end, Winckelmann means the architecture of supremacy, means Hitler. He is Winckelmann's true heir. And this always under the cynical appeal to humanism, classicism, and antiquity. The architect was always swayed by the notion of power, because pride, triumph over gravity, will to power were to become visible in a building. *Architecture is a kind of eloquence of power in shapes,* and the highest feeling of power finds expression in what has *grandiose style.*

All these architects of displays of power and temple sites of the movement were constructed by Winckelmann, but not by me, who had long known the terror of the dungeon and had etched it on copper.

When I look at the statues of an Arno Breker, I recognize in them the handwriting of Winckelmann as I do in the colossal structures of the fascists, which today, in accordance with the law, are classed as worthy of preservation as memorials: a park for memories of horror and fish-and-fries booths. Here as well as there, it's strictly a matter of teaching rotting bones to tremble. Breker's metallic body language, hidden behind the aura of mythical and divine shapes, seeks dignity and classicality, beauty, youth, will, strength. Nude bodies, like those that heated up Winckelmann, carry the titles *Blossoming, Expectation, Surrender.* That is armament in a Winckelmann costume. Monumentalism and the gesture of superiority, cult character and the inclusion of emblems of supremacy, the transtemporal claim of marble and granite, the rebirth of classicism from the spirit of Winckelmann:

that repulsive junk with lanky, broad-shouldered, slim-hipped, steadfast, naked men with bulging eyebrows and energetic chins, that rigid musculature, that pathos of body, that disgusting fuss about power, energy, dynamics, nobility, loyalty, bravery, duty, obedience, and toughness is to be blamed solely on that *finocchio*.

The piously antique character of an expression of art is the transmission of the divine to the human. So the figures are not idealized human beings but human beings as the embodiment of ideals. They are not created for the spirit of the times but show timelessness, and the past is revealed as the present experienced in duration. The soul of the artist is reflected in what he creates. Whenever I glorify anything, then it is beauty. The beauty of the human being, the beauty of the human body. I strive for the ideal, humane image of man. The deeper the penetration into the essence of appearance, the closer the work comes into the epoch of timeless validity. An artwork of rank begins first with the spiritualization of matter. If the Greek creations reproduced the transtemporal essence of characters, then the Roman contribution aimed at a verity not known up to that time. The Greeks succeeded in totally breaking the human figure free. The contribution of the Greeks in the development of sculpture presents a unique high point in this spiritualization of form. The harmony of all forces is what I call classic. Classicism is the expression of absolute harmony in the universe. Everything has its firm place in that, a harmonious order.

Now just guess who that is by: Winckelmann or Breker, who has the nerve to refer to Michelangelo and Bernini and dream of becoming an important architect.

Winckelmann's cult of beauty lets the swastika banner wave over the Acropolis, subordinates even the military objectives of antiquity, brings about Hitler's gassed art-hygienic vision of horror with a reference to the marble sculptures of the Greeks, which supposedly lend artistic expression to the longing of a people for racist perfection. By 1934 Hitler and Speer develop a ruins law whereby important buildings are to be constructed so gigantic and so violent that in a distant future they could weather away to picturesque ruins that might be reminiscent of Greek antiquity. Building materials and construction is discussed, and Speer prepares sketches that depict the planned buildings half crumbled and grown over with ivy. They were to be ruins of a past that would not vanish in order, as Hitler said, *to loom like the cathedrals of our past into the millennia of the future.* That is an aestheticism of horror that minutely describes all hideousness and that effectively dresses up decay sensually. The work of art is consummated in its detachment from life. The means of these *words of stone* are as simple as they are effective: the right angle, the large number, ornamentation and mass. But in the end everything leads to crematorium architecture. Winckelmann's cult of beauty leads on a direct path to the gas chamber.

Hitler himself, always with a sketch pad within reach, prepared to capture the ideas of a potential Michelangelo in an instant, liked to say in his closest circle that he would one day retire from politics and be only what he had always wanted to become: a great architect.

In his speeches on art and architecture he again and again referred to Winckelmann, not by chance. Art should offer only the pure and the beautiful. And when after 1945 the diehards discovered modernity, they complained about the loss of the core that Winckelmann and his Nazi heirs had provided.

In the final analysis, however, it is only a matter of disguising war plans with architectural plans, for the urge to build and to destroy go here hand in hand. Anyone who looks at Speer's architectural plans today, at once sees the bombed cities that Hitler stubbornly refused to look at. No building that he ever thought of erecting had a firmer foundation than his delusion. And he had Winckelmann's historic junk in mind.

Winckelmann's system of theories rests exclusively on contemplation and observation; I, on the other hand, as an imaginary architect aim at a spatialization of history, for the question of space is a question of reality. In my person the relationship between architect and God the Creator is reversed, so to speak. The artist is not called upon to mimic antiquity stupidly, but with a reflection of the art of ages past to find his own standpoint and become creatively active. *Inventio* no longer pertains to a model outside of art, such as Nature, but to free artistic invention and its relationship to the lost past.

An artist gets by somehow by repeatedly conjuring up memory and seeking a dialogue with the shades. That doesn't occur without resignation. By that I don't mean a mystic, distanced resignation but one conscious, flopping on the long rope of love, practiced with open eyes, for it is the only one of our emotions that cannot possibly be feigned. No one can escape his fate, but the lot not drawn remains a powerless piece of paper.

Anyway, I survived the main vile person in my life. While the successful Winckelmann seems to have died finally with his century, I dream as an inferior through the ages.

Struck down by malarial fever, I see myself as Arcangeli entering room *Numero 10* on the third story of the municipal guest house on Peter's Square in Trieste: the room of my great adversary. I still had his words in my ear: "Anyone who distances himself from Winckelmann, distances himself from Greek culture."

But I turned the German's words against him: Anyone who removes Winckelmann removes philhellenism and the ludicrous reverence of what is Greek that has seized all of Europe.

The German Winckelmann: the awakener of antiquity. Father of archaeology. A life for Apollo. Don't make me laugh. Nothing but a schoolmaster of Greek culture.

The vain and fluttering moth was not satisfied, Leonardo tells in his *Favole,* to be able to fly around comfortably. Bewitched by the flames of a candle, it decided to fly into them. But its wings were zapped by the light, and the moth fell singed down to the base of the candelabra.

The German peacock with his furunculous neck, the slightly swollen skin, and the inflamed bristles on the back of his neck stands before me, driven by the power of attraction to male bordellos, dark houses, low dives with clean boys that I had promised him, I, Arcangeli the suck-up, medium-sized, dark, a braid of twisted hair hanging down behind, in my thirty-eighth year but still with my Apollo physique, *a man of Italian taste* about whom James Boswell, may he rest in peace, had warned his countrymen: the angel of death of the Last Judgment. Arcangeli, as I imagine him: rich-yellow trousers, siskin-green jacket, cinnamon-colored gentleman's vest, bright red scarf instead of a jabot, and then those white teeth that must have seemed to Winckelmann like the maw of a beast of prey. And the *cazzo* Winckelmann: black silk hose, pants of black leather with silver clasps, white linen shirt with wide cuffs and gold buttons, the hairless chest revealed, ready to be carved, stabbed. Once more his gaze goes out the window down to the harbor, before him the water with the barques, masts and sails, each of which seemed to him to be a bridge to faraway wonders. He looks at the city, about which the people say: Here there is an archangel who takes away the life of travelers.

The *stronzetto* Winckelmann, childishly intent on fame, on applause, on being well known and greeted, remembers the rambling walks at the side of Arcangeli Piranesi, who accompanied him stubbornly though the streets with their bustle of hawkers, sailors, soldiers, priests, and females, across the wagon-rattled Corso, the Molo San Carlo lively with mares, the Aquedotto, through the green plane-tree lanes of Sant'Andrea peopled with rosebushes, the oak grove of Boschetto, or to Servola, on the right the sea, villas and gardens on the left. Arcangeli, too, has a weakness for radiance and color, for everything that is rich, elegant, and dazzling. He, too, seeks splendor, comfort, and being served. The German gives an impression of being young. Had he not once boasted that he dated his age for the first time from the hour when he had awakened in a shabby *albergo* in Rome! He was to have it as he figured it out: According to his reckoning he was twelve years old, going on thirteen, just as old as the innocent youths he had murdered by fondling, seducing, corrupting them. Goethe to Eckermann on February 16, 1827: *One encounters him occasionally kind of groping along.*

To stock up with the necessary small change, I pawned a little gold ring with a Jesuit priest, Bosizio, who fixed me up with a small loan. The tragedy of the last act can begin: the grand scholar of art and antiquity and the miserable cook. I know that in my pocket is the cord, picked up for three *soldi* from the small shopkeeper Marianna Derin, that I will place around the scabies-covered neck of that creep, in my hand the knife—a Venetian product—will that betray me, will it betray the Venetian Piranesi?—with a black horn handle and dull tin decorations, obtained for nine groschen in the cellar shop of Pfneisl et Comp. The archangel's flaming sword of justice. It lies well in my hand.

The German sees Arcangeli's knife, and he seems to be about to say with his always slightly husky voice: "Am I, who looked into the face of Apollo, to become a common animal for slaughter by a tramp?" The suck-up Arcangeli, the Venetian knife, and the hyacinth sea. The screaming gulls that hang low over the water. The German *stronzo* Winckelmann grabs the knife by its blade and holds it with all his strength and with his other hand at my chest he grips my vest and shirt. We wrestle with one another and fall to the floor, and I close my eyes because I don't want to see what I will now do. Then I strike, two, three times I strike with all my strength. Noble simplicity and quiet grandeur collapse wretchedly, dripping with dirty green blood as otherwise only stabbed dragons exude. And the sea, the sea gleams hyacinthean. The louder the *cazzone* Winckelmann screams, the less he is heard. He sees the skeletons of the ships gleam and smooth male backs bent over nets like over good fortune. But beyond the ships he no longer sees the boys. His death throes last seven hours, and no surgeon can help him. The German always remains conscious, laments, and wants to launch into his favorite song "I sing to thee with heart and mouth," but the surgeon Antonio Albrizzi commands him to be quiet. Anyway, there's time enough to make his last will and testament, to receive the blessings of the church— but which, the Lutheran or the Roman?—and to forgive his murderer. A Capuchin monk gives him so-called spiritual comfort. Seven hours of vengeance and gossipy sympathy in the face of the hyacinthean sea until the enemy's eyes from Stendal in the Altmark fade and for the last time saliva runs from his mouth. Toward four o'clock in the afternoon it happens. The German Winckelmann, who considered himself a chosen one, stretches his hand out toward the surgeon, stares into a pockmarked face— he shudders, for he has dedicated his life to beauty, only to beauty, and his hand reaches into a dark, shapeless cloud. He lays his head on his knee, trembles, and becomes silent. But that is not death after a short and quick pain, such as the gentlemen from Weimar envisioned for himself: nothing there of the rays of eternal beauty. A slaughter victim in the wind of misfortune, sentenced by my hand. Cuts on both hands, a wound near his left nipple, two deep wound channels, one of which has punctured the left lung, and two other stab wounds that had damaged the diaphragm and the abdominal wall. Five pounds of blood, it says in the autopsy report signed by the three doctors, had built up in the abdominal cavity. *These two wounds, because of the large and inevitable loss of blood, because of the impossibility of breathing, because of the injury to the stomach and its entrance into the chest cavity, we judged to be absolutely fatal and as the principal cause of death.*

Now he could have sung, this monkey of coarse nature—he had after all seen service in an itinerant boys' choir at deaths. But he didn't sing. And now, too, there was no Anton Raphael Mengs left to stand by him. *That happens when you claim to visit emperors and to collect treasures,* Lessing wrote to Nicolai. Winckelmann was interred in a charnel house of a brotherhood. And when that burial place was rearranged after many years and subsequently had to be enlarged, Winckelmann's ashes wound up in the common charnel house, where they now lie, though unidentified and forgotten. However, it is remarkable that it never occurred to Cardinal Albani, his patron and heir, to have a gravestone set for Winckelmann. Not until about fifty years later did the Trieste jurist and antiquarian Domenico de Rossetti campaign in his monograph *Joh. Winckelmann's Last Week of Life* for contributions for a memorial, which today stands in the small classicist temple beneath the cupola of San Giusto, a work of the pupil of Canova, Antonio Bosa. On my most recent visit to Trieste the temple had fallen in the *orto lapidario* to a building site, and not even the rickety custodian knew anything about Winckelmann. *Sic transit gloria mundi.* His contour remains for no one. The havoc was understood and judged. There was no country that was broad enough, no water that was deep enough, and no mountain range that might have been desolate enough to protect Winckelmann from me. To take revenge on him for Rome I would even have been ready to set the sea ablaze. I spat at Winckelmann's corpse and my spittle was as thick as mortar.

I had to flee, for I had killed. Arcangeli fled with blood-spattered shirt across the Piazza of Trieste. Without having been stopped he reached the mountains and went on smugglers' paths across the border toward Capo d'Istria. On the main highway a road supervisor advised me to avoid Capo d'Istria because a reward had already been offered for me there and instead to spend the night in a farmhouse so I could get to Isola the following day. But I found a different haven, the name of which I didn't even know. There Arcangeli met a locksmith from Trieste who recognized me and advised me to take off as quickly as I could, since the search for Arcangeli was on everywhere. A sailor gave me an old seaman's jacket and a hat, for which I turned over to him my short jacket. So disguised, Arcangeli took the path over the mountains and wandered around until he came to the main highway not far from Fiume that leads to Laibach. I kept walking on that road without really thinking of the great danger. I passed the military garrison and guard without being stopped until I came to Planina. There Arcangeli met a soldier with a drummer who held me until their absent officer would return. I spent three or four hours at the main police station. And then since the officer considered me suspicious because I couldn't produce a passport, he sent me well guarded to Adelsberg, where Arcangeli confessed his crime before the district captain. Arcangeli was immediately taken on a wagon to Trieste, handed over to the chief sheriff and locked up in Criminal Prison No. 2. On July 20, 1768, Arcangeli had to go on the wheel on Peter's Square, directly across the street from the inn where I had done Winckelmann in. Of course, the murderer was spared public humiliation since with her kiss of farewell his beloved, a girl named Serafina, pushed into his mouth a small nut that contained a deadly poison. Arcangeli died on the spot without a word.

With a heavy head I woke up at last in the Hotel *Locanda Grande* on the Piazza San Pietro, which today is the Piazza dell'Unità in the center of Trieste. A freshly renovated, four-story building, the best address in the city—Casanova stayed here and Emperor Joseph II—forty rooms are available, and roomy stables, in addition the so-called Casino of Nobles, a night café. My room was on the second floor: Number 10.

Slowly I came to and respected the fever anew because it brought me dreams that turned my innermost feelings inside out and brought the truth to light. Shut up in my boneless body, I believed it was sufficient to live on as before. I tried to assess my past and my guilt with the measure that I was forced to discover arduously in my life gone wrong. Suddenly I saw how many years separated me from the moment when I had been happy for the first time. As though drunk I drank deeply into me with eyes wide open the vision of the end of my adversary.

I learned this upward glance from the birds. Again I gathered together all the strength that still was available to me and brought myself to a final cycle. And gnashing my teeth I had to admit: These structures were Greek. But in my notes I avoided every single reference to that. I knew that my chronic kidney ailment did not leave me much time. The picturesquely done drawings, preliminarily drawn with chalk, almost without corrections, gone over in detail with reed pens and enhanced with several washes in their light and shadow effects, cannot find their like in my work. Where once I was content with casual contours, where I selected out of a chaos of knowledge in my work, here I completed the picture on drawing paper and left it up to the engraver to transfer it. Since I was aware of the obvious weaknesses of my son Francesco, slighted by nature, I wrote down the process for him in detail just in case. These twenty etchings were again to be a masterwork: a summation of my artistic accomplishments and pioneering, forward-looking interpretation in one. It was the harmony of ruins and wilderness.

My testament.

The cycle was wholly meant for observation, was an appeal to the fantasy of the expert and the admirer. I shaped the three Doric temples from every possible point of view, perhaps with a secret penchant for the unspoiled gravity of the so-called basilica, whose precipitously tapering columns, pressing closely to one another, whose excessively formulated capitals, and whose low silhouette appealed to my sense of what is moderate and what is curious at the same time. My drawings indicate that I made use of the same reed pen, the same brownish ink, and also the same rough manner of depiction as in the sketches at Pompeii. Let researchers talk here about a style of old age, for all I care. All the same, this style is kept in the spatial visions that roused my imagination once more in all the magic of the illusion of Baroque stage perspectives—far-reaching panoramas, drastically reduced exterior views of the temples that let the successively terraced travertine columns appear like forward and backward staired parts of a bizarre wall of rock, but above all attain ever-new views through the trunks of those petrified magic forests. The shepherds and boy cowherders, the water buffaloes, swine, and pack animals, the few gentlemen of rank that on the fourth plate stare from horseback mistrustfully at the rows of columns they find eerie, are placed about the ruins in their natural size, and the temples themselves also gain their grandeur from the contrast to the empty plain that surrounds them on all sides—like my soul. The column drums press, outlined sharply in every unevenness, right up to the observer, the temple rears past the amazed observer so that he, between the rows of columns that stand around him closely in deep shadow, glimpses even more distant rows, and so the impression must arise that he is standing in an unreal forest whose edges are transformed into silver. As always I have analyzed the structures precisely and worked out every unusual detail exactly: the protruding swellings of the ovolo moldings on the basilica, the Ionic-like entrance hall of the Temple of Hera, the varying pattern of the interior walls. On the basis of my experience in life, I squeezed the lower proportions in relation to their ambience and to their residents in order, probably in vain again, to point out the characteristic features to which this temple owes its beauty. The situation of the ruins, the play of light and shadow on the breached walls that I so often exaggerated, the vitality of the stone all contributed to the poetic transfiguration of the place.

And something else: I did not capitulate to that immeasurably overestimated Winckelmann. On the contrary, I laid the foundations beyond him for a new understanding of Greek architecture that was no longer determined by fashionable Hellenism but acknowledged the original artistic spirit. I was aware of the import of this discovery: that the main features of my theory of art allowed me to comprehend the most perfect architecture, whereas my adversaries had failed with their trendy neo-Grecian thoughts. Besides, I realized that that *cazzone* Winckelmann was no artist. He relied too much on immortality. But the artist knows that he has only a short span of life and that the day will come when he will have to pass through the wall of oblivion—and all his days he would like nothing more than to leave his scratches on that wall. The *cazzo* Winckelmann never understood that.

The difference between Winckelmann and me is very simple: A scholar may be someone who has learned a lot. But a genius is someone from whom humankind has something to learn. Art is not only there exclusively to produce beauty. The opposite of the sublime is not the ugly, as Winckelmann alleged, but what is pleasing, which he constantly propagandized. Besides, everything beautiful submits to the compulsion of having to be presented as unity and harmony. Ugliness, on the other hand, is daring. What is generally pleasing without being interesting is beautiful, says the philosopher. And the poet says: *Sorrow is based on what is fair, The joy in what's ugly is always there.* Consequently, anything that is without interest generally displeases us.

But what excites interest?

Not what is pleasant but deviation?

My *Carceri* grew out of my passionate pleasure in deviation. They are the product of humiliation and hate. Artistic conscious-ness, once the infinite source of joy, has become the inexhaustible arsenal of the tools of torture. Not noble simplicity and quiet grandeur but only what is ugly reveals the art of new themes: the bursting of boundaries, empty ideality, dismantling and deform-ing, disorienting, sensual irreality, isolation and anxiety, darkness. What is ugly is the union of what is horrifying and what is idiotic.

Therefore, particularly with my *Carceri*, I did infinitely more for the development of art than all the depictions of Apollo heaped up together.

In the autumn of 1778 I returned to Rome to my bleak and desperate present as a dying man. My scars had meanwhile become so numerous that there was no place left for a badge of honor. Sleep seemed to me to be the only thing I could succeed in, but that too was a failure. Again and again that thirst for sleep. Finally, I was tortured by a frequently recurring dream in which someone tried to hack off my hands. I could never find out exactly who was involved: Angelica, Winckelmann, or one of my critics, who were my greatest abusers. They always hid their faces as though in a fog. Then again I saw myself as a rat on the ship *Nosferatus* before I rolled myself up on my deathbed and crossed my skinny legs.

But one thing did become clear to me: No guilt is forgotten as long as your conscience knows about it. But I don't want to linger with those wretches who thwarted me. Why do I worry today about whose dead mouth spurts criticism? Voltaire, with whom I share the year of my death anyway, once said: *We have only two days to live; it isn't worth the effort to spend them by crawling before despicable rogues.*

Sometimes I dreamed that our entire world was flying like a colorful, firm children's ball in a marvelous arc back into the merciless grip of a heathen god. But maybe it's not at all a matter of the pain or of the joy of people but much more of how light and shadow play on a living body or how the most ridiculous trifles at a very specific moment collect harmonically in a singular and incomparable way.

I remember my last dream:

Winckelmann had written to me. The effeminately perfumed

note began—as with Angelica—with the words *My dear friend and copperplate engraver* and was full of the most toadying and re-pulsive praise of me. The *cazzone* lauded my knowledge, praised my abilities, called me finally the greater, by far the more impor-tant, the more genial of the two of us. It was the most malicious form of vengeance that can possibly be imagined. Nothing worse could have happened to me than to be celebrated by this vain fop in a song of praise.

Bathed in sweat, I awoke at my own scream. An attack of un-controlled rage followed. With foaming mouth I struck about me, tore up some of my etchings, flung away whatever I could get my hands on. The shock was so elementary, however, that from ex-haustion I soon fell asleep again, and again I dreamed of Winckelmann. I dreamed he had taken up residence in my house only one floor higher and, in order to be able to trample around on me and to drive me completely crazy, that he had transformed himself into that armor-plated rhinoceros that Dürer had cut into wood. We don't understand animals, but I dreamed how Dürer came upon his rhinoceros. I dreamed of Winckelmann, how he worked as a printer and translator in Lisbon. He collected reports about the travels of the Portuguese to the African coast and sent them to Germany, where they served as a basis for some latest news. I dreamed of how Winckelmann wrote a letter to a friend in Nuremberg, in which he announced the arrival of a rhinoceros that the king of Cambodia had sent to King Manuel I of Portugal and that the latter had had shipped by sea to Roma—as a gift for the pope. But the animal, the sculpture of which even today can be seen on an oriel of the façade of the Tower of Belém, did not arrive at its destination alive. On the way it was shipwrecked and was washed ashore on an Italian beach. After it was recovered, its skin was stuffed and it finally arrived in that condition at the addressee. But Winckelmann added to his letter to Nuremberg a sketch of the animal. Letter and drawing, I dreamed, came into the possession of Dürer, who immortalized the animal.

Admittedly, Winckelmann's letter released in me a certain self-doubt. But it never occurred to me to dwell on it, even though at this opportunity I must confess that the terrible slaughter of the German in Trieste induced a certain shiver in me. After all, I'm not a monster but only the living proof that someone who wants only to do good inevitably drags behind himself the rattail of Hell.

Winckelmann and I: We were like scorpions encircled by fire. What could we do other than sting one another to death?

Often my dreams are nightly processes that are carried out on a revolving stage and in which there is a judgment about everything that one had become guilty of during the day. How you accuse yourself! How you condemn yourself! Every night you discover yourself somewhat more exactly on that revolving stage.

But at the end of my dream the rhinoceros suddenly had Angelica's facial features. And there was an odor of Angelica, and there was movement just as lascivious and charming as Angelica.

I still yearn for the tenderness of her arm, for the hills of her shoulders, for her arrogantly curved lips, for the melancholy forlornness of her bushy blackness, and for that unfathomable place between her ear and nape that is as white as sliced bread. A flourish of her smile, an oblique blink of her eye could disarm me.

All the stairs resound from Angelica's step.

Angelica always had her small smile for me, and when in my presence her name sounded in a gathering, it was each time for me a black blow.

Angelica, the shadows of your unsteady voice pursue me everywhere.

Unforgotten, the gestures with which you wove your braid.

I'm still in love with this woman and can't get away from her. Maybe I'm now at that second stage of love, which takes nourishment from the memory of the first stage. It is that second stage of love into which one enters as soon as, full of despair, you feel that love dies. Why did Angelica never hold my hand in sleep? After all, love means nothing more than to be completely at someone's mercy. Between lovers rules of the game quickly come into being, of which they are not aware and that yet are valid—and that they may not overstep. Angelica's game rule was that I was not to hold her hand while she was asleep. On the other hand, I had adopted the secret game rule that my name should never be connected to sadness. But that failed miserably. Since I became aware of that, I wished that the years would drop away from me like dandruff. But it didn't happen. The consciousness of my own misery in no way reconciled me to her own misery.

It cost me a lot of effort to realize that my life had become no stable house, which as an architect I had dreamed for myself. Even in this I had failed as an architect, for I had not succeeded in placing my life on a firm foundation. I built on Angelica as though on sand.

Angelica Pasquini: I still carry her name around in me like an open knife. I yearn for her as you long for something that you have lost irretrievably. And just as Angelica had become for me something irretrievable, something that as past was always vital but as something present was untouchable, in my thoughts she never lost her corporeality and still became more and more a legend, a myth written on quickly bleaching paper that, locked in an expensive box, had been sunk in the quaking fundament of my life. The question that decided everything remained unanswered for always: Why did I have to meet her? Was it chance? Do such stories say something, aside from the fact that they happen? The sparrows of chance had settled on my shoulders, and I spoke to Angelica. Since then I have often wondered whether an event does not become all the more significant and momentous, the more coincidences are necessary for its coming into being. Not necessity but coincidence is full of enchantment. *If love is to be unforgettable, then from the first moment on coincidences must settle on it like birds on the shoulders of St. Francis of Assisi,* says the poet.

But between such considerations came the merciless knowledge of my own baseness and the insight that my thoughts and words strove aloft in vain as long as my action stumbled along on such leaden feet. Perhaps I expected too much of Angelica. Perhaps I should have asked from her only as much as she could handle in harmony with her deepest self-illusions.

Angelica: High as the vault of a cathedral was the sound of her laughter. That gave her love something of weightlessness. But I made the mistake of considering her something without which my life was not possible. Perhaps happiness is the desire for repetition. I don't know. I know only one thing: A human life takes place only once, and therefore we'll never be able to determine which of our decisions were good and which bad because we can always decide only once. No second, third, or fourth life is given us.

I still believe in the miracle of fidelity. It is a mistake when one prevents the happy moments of life from being complete and thus from attaining their perfection. *Infidelity:* what an intemperate word! The hour is not far away when the most unsparing novels will be completely unreadable because they will have only a risible effect. People won't understand why we seriously argue so about infidelity in such a way. They will look upon that problem as an idée fixe of poets and bards, an inexplicable idée fixe like honor and the faithfulness of women.

In my dream I bent over the *Carceri* as a rhinoceros and suddenly discovered in the cross-hatching a Madonna. Instantly a crazy idea took hold of me. Just imagine that, instead of pulling a drawn figure out of an etching, someone would succeed in stepping into the picture himself. I did it. I bent deeper over my depiction of dungeons and concentrated all my will on the one thought: of diving into the picture and disappearing in it. I seemed to be like the apostle who sets about climbing out of the boat and walking on the water. So that etching lay before me and expected me. I took heart, tore myself away from life, and stepped into the etching. A wonderful feeling! Cool, still air steeped with incense, and I became a living part of the picture, and everything about me came alive. The silhouettes of prisoners and torturers moved on the path. Light shown through, the windlasses turned, and the timbers cracked. I discovered my Madonna. She had the features of Angelica. Immediately, and on the spot, I was in love with that Madonna and remembered my first great love: a Madonna with a blue crown. Behind her at some distance two men between columns stood and whispered. I crept nearer and recognized Winckelmann and one of my critics. I listened to their conversation. It concerned the price of a dagger with a Venetian handle. The Madonna had elongated, tenderly half-closed eyes; her gown was subdued in bluish-red and veiled orange hues. On her brow hovered a slight haze, an undulating mist. Honey-sweet darkness drifted toward me, and I peered into the depth of a high window breaking through the black background. There sand-colored clouds drifted in a greenish blue sky; chasmed cliffs reared up to them, between them a pale path wound. Farther below, shabby huts could be seen. For a moment it seemed as though a point of light flamed up in one of them. While I looked through this window of air, I felt that my Madonna smiled, but when I turned my gaze quickly toward her, I could no longer see her smile. Only very slightly was the shadowed corner of her barely closed lips raised. I devoured the face of that beautiful woman with my eyes, shrank back from her, and spread my arms out wide as though I were about to fly to her. There was an aroma of myrrh and wax and a slight trace of lemon. The Madonna stood before me, tall, graceful, glowing from within. And I understood that a miracle had taken place. Calmly the woman adjusted her gown, let her hand sink into a basket, and handed me a small lemon. Without turning my glance from her lively eyes I accepted the fruit from her hand. Then I turned again to the window. There on the pale path between the cliffs walked dark silhouettes in cowls with lanterns in their hands. In the background gleamed an enticing surface of water. I could no longer move my head and sank like a fly in honey, jerked and stiffened, and felt how my clothing turned into printer's ink and cat's blood and began to dry on the sheet. I had become a part of my etching. Directly in front of me further dungeons opened, full of an air that I would not be able to breathe from now on. Only a moment more and my etching would have sucked me into it forever. I would have gone into its background and would have lived on in the prison, able neither to return to the world nor to press on into a new realm: stiffened as an etched part of the picture.

My dream of the rhinoceros made me aware of my greatest talent in the last moments of my life: the talent of jealousy. Suddenly I realized that I had been just as jealous of Winckelmann and his successes as of Angelica's uncounted lovers, who all had only one name: Winckelmann. Jealousy swam in my body like a fish full of air. I remembered my friends, who never grew weary of explaining to me that Angelica was not the only woman on earth. Rome teemed with seductive women who were only waiting to finally be seduced. But my friends had understood nothing: Angelica was the only woman for me. She was my last chance. From the beginning. So in my miserable breast burns the bitter flame, Angelica.

One day Angelica left me for good. In spite of all the humiliations and self-denial that had gone before, for me her decision was completely unexpected and struck me like a fatal blow. She closed her hand as though she were keeping the sun in it. Today I no longer know what happened to my wife, when and where and how she died. I have forgotten dates and circumstances. But not this woman. Thank God that she was not an artist herself. There is nothing more terrible than a marriage of artists. If there are two artists, they destroy themselves mutually. Or the woman submits and is destroyed. Or the man submits and is destroyed. The artist must be alone. Against the world, alone and lonely. Against everyone and against everything. In spite of everything that Angelica did to me, in my heart I have built her a memorial that is indestructible. Of course, today the discovery does surprise me that I never felt the wish to die at Angelica's side.

Angelica: The birdlike flutter of her soul.

Angelica: Had she limped, her limping would have made dancers appear like cripples.

Angelica: With every sentence that we said to one another we took farewell from each other, but your name remains nevertheless engraven in my memory. It remains an abscessing scar on my soul.

Angelica: Where were you in that dark hour when the critics fell upon me like vultures to tear me to pieces? Where were you? At my side, as you had once sworn: in good and in bad days? No, you betrayed me to my critics and went like a challenge cup through their beds.

And if you believe now that I would thus besmirch her memory, then I assure you that there is no memory to besmirch because no one remembers anything: least of all Angelica Pasquini. She exists only because I tell about her. My life gone wrong is a constant farewell from things and people who only too often did not give my bitter greeting the least attention.

With my dream of the rhinoceros I had arrived at my last shore. I speak from the heart when I assure you that I prefer the bucolic peace of these valleys with their aroma of pasture, these steep paths, these old, humble dwellings that, as though from the void, seem fixed directly behind a bend in the path at world's end, to the varied and perfect spectacle of these last coasts with crags that in the intensity of their red hues are reflected sharply against the blue of the heavens and mirrored below in the blue of the sea.

The completion of my works no longer interested me, although I worked to my last breath, as I had been accustomed to do doing from my childhood. When I knew that that life was coming to an end as it is falsified in history books, I called out for the volumes of my beloved Livy instead of for a doctor or a priest.

In addition I had myself served Tacchino all'Arcangeli, knowing full well that every bite would turn to ashes in my throat. But one does not die well on an empty stomach.

A doctor sees a human being in his entire weakness, as the lawyer does a human being in his entire baseness, and the theologian a human being in his entire stupidity. All of them are bent on training a human being. And in this regard religion is the greatest instrument for training that can possibly be imagined. The Muslims are trained to turn toward Mecca five times a day; Christians are trained to cross themselves constantly; and doctors train people to swallow pills and to trust their gibberish that still is of no help; but nothing helps because doctors know as little about human beings as do theologians about the so-called soul.

Books have always been for me the most faithful and reliable companions and would be also in the life beyond. With books I returned to the dreams of Roman grandeur and was transformed into the most significant architect that the Eternal City ever had.

For I, only I myself, had once more built that ancient Rome in all its sunken and forgotten *magnificenza:* even if only with the cold needle.

There is no architecture without hope. New worlds want to be dreamed up. A dream always preceded great architecture. No architecture is therefore possible without the gift of dream, without the grace of vision.

But for petty-minded persons and nitpickers among historians on November 9—in the same year as Voltaire, Rousseau, and Linné—I died not unwillingly of the ailments that I had endured stoically for years, although as a sick man I had myself gotten control of my ailments, particularly in my mind. Afterward my life's capital was exhausted, and I'm living on credit. My last will and testament contained the behest to place me on my belly in the coffin. I died in the same condition in which I was born. Since that hour I have become boundless and unpredictable for myself. I laughed at my megalomania until I cried.

No one yet has found the word for one who enters death. On that day I saw a lark outside my window. It stared at me fixedly. The lark is a bird of which Leonardo da Vinci relates in his *Bestiario* that when it is brought to someone who is about to die, it turns its head aside and never looks at him. But if the sick man is going to survive, then the bird doesn't let him out of its sight and sees to it that all evil avoids him.

Dying is a trifle for the one who has enough fantasy. There are moments of our existence in which time and scope deepen and the feeling of our existence experiences a heightening into immensity.

Voltaire, Rousseau, Linné, and I.

It was our century, it was mine, but not Winckelmann's! He

thought of himself as a so-called great man, but so-called great men are no longer men at all but only consequences.

I am one of those men who are killed in a mysterious way, but whose death doesn't take place at once, instead possibly needs centuries. In me the word in the Book of Revelation is fulfilled, where it says: *And in those days men shall seek death, and shall in no wise find it; and they shall desire to die, and death fleeth from them.* Only growing old is the shape of death that we experience every day. And through all the years during which I could not die, I arrived at the conviction that it is impossible to really imagine death. But the situation of one who thinks of death is ridiculous, because his unrest, which concerns something simultaneously so very vague and concrete and that therefore sets boundaries for nothing, is a product of his quixotic imagination. All great men longed for death. I know that from a letter of Boccaccio's.

Life lived has an inclination to simplify. As preparation for death it lasts just as long as is necessary. In the end, you live only to prepare yourself for being dead. But we know nothing of death because we don't experience it. We know nothing but play our roles. The death of others helps us live. Perhaps the fear of death lets us love our work, but nothing is as strange and as dark as the blow that fells each of us.

Age crept with the same simplicity into my life with which a cat comes through an open door. When life nighs to its end, many do not know where it has been. The longer I live, the less most events seem significant enough to me to give them my attention. Only someone who gets old receives an appropriate idea of life. The basic characteristic of great age is that of being disappointed: Illusions vanish, one has recognized the futility and emptiness of all the glories of the world, one has seen that there is little behind most desires and yearnings, and one thus gradually arrives at an insight into the piteousness and preposterousness of existence. One's earlier life furnishes, so to speak, the text, but old age provides a commentary on it that only then reveals correctly the sense and linkages of the text. Of course, I cannot forgive or forget, for that would mean simply to throw the experiences I had out the window. Still, growing old is itself thoroughly immoral.

Every day I wonder: Why am I outside of myself? I see my life as a consistent diversion from my life. It is always the same, and my participation in the world seems to decline steadily. Having set out on an endless path, I seem to myself like someone whom this path must convince about its endlessness. And a mutilated sky hangs above me from which fairly large chunks fall on me. I can do what I want. I have long since given up the thought of my so-called soul, for the thing about the so-called soul is nothing but a preposterous fad of clerics. What counts is only the horribly choking weariness that forces my temples into a vise. From that my face received its wrinkles and furrows, my beard and hair turned gray, my stride became ever heavier. In addition came the dislike for the body that I had, and for its desires that constantly ready the knife. If I set all my experiences in a row, in the end everything is falsehood and lie, deception, infamy, abyss. I am amazed at the ridiculous crippling of my crippled brain. Ridiculous the many long tedious years that have deceived me, that have condemned me, that now laugh at me and spit at me. My whole life tossed on the manure heap. It is only natural that a man may not come to terms with his death. I too have succumbed to this desire, but my life stopped at the instant of my death, as it were. The same day and the same night have been repeated thousands and thousands of times, without moving a step forward. The stream of time passes over me, and my soul is laden with a black stone that looks like a nun. Since then my path leads through time, edged with milestones of futility, accompanied by the ruins of my rotting illusions and the shabby background from the junk room, no, from the leaden dungeon of my hopes and desires. Out of them I built my filigree building of salvation, constructed on hollow stage planks. On them I play the slapstick comedy of my life gone wrong. The supposedly grand and raging spectacle. We stage it, incessantly, in our imagination, before a raptly listening public that in reality wants nothing more than to display its furs and pearls.

We never know exactly under what memory our imprisoned mind digs. Memories kill you. You ought to wait until they are completely covered with mud.

November 9, 1778!

I noted that falsified date on my suspenders.

These nights, in which my face swelled up unendurably under the scornful glow of the stars, were the longest in my life. I realized that I had to forget how it could have been with me. Perhaps most awkward is that it still always continues somehow. Only after my alleged death did I, the figure, become form. For I discovered a gap in my being out of which I could now crawl completely.

Now you want to know how I lived the entire time after that?

From the mange of this bankrupt world, from the salt of planets and from the darkness during the day. In order to walk around, a ghost must first have died, or at least have been born. All the days matter: as though I had only been dreamed until I arrived in a dead bay of time with a body that was blotched with sickness like a bed pad. Faced with languishing away, I waited for hours for the easing up of my pains and for the first time comprehended the first rule of architecture: that Nature knows no straight line and no equilibrium. In the hour of the pale pus fluid, a man recognizes himself: how he creeps into himself because he wants out of himself.

From now on my hours sprang over other times. I give myself more time to die and give death more time to live. Since then I've been waiting for something to happen, anything paltry and disappointing that could be useful to my loneliness. One can ban death anyway only into the story of one's own life gone wrong.

I'm talking about it as though it had been yesterday. Yesterday is not long past, but already too long. Not what I was and how I acted will be passed on to my descendants, rather what was added in the way of commentaries in the galleries of memory. The details unmask the myths. My epoch was not my sphere of activity but only the stony ground on which my miserable physical existence suffered privations—it was, of course, only the unimportant part of my Self. In ordinary life you aren't at all what you are in the heightened moments of creation. Sometimes I am myself amazed at how I was able to endure all that and to create. What is later gladly called epoch is, of course, first just everyday stuff, and nothing grows old more quickly than the gaze of one epoch at a preceding one.

How quickly what is lost in the past comes into being. I was not yet old and had already forgotten my life. I wanted to preserve my solitude and still came into contact with all the rubbish that the world chokes up. I flung my etchings into outer space. They traveled unending stretches on vibrations that I wakened blithely with my hand. Since then they circle the world, and one day they will fall from the sky like rain. I settled down on my own pile of ruins and am plagued by the desires of my premature old age. I treat my memories like a father his numerous descendants: They come to keep him company, especially at night, and make him laugh or brood darkly to himself.

Men have died at their appointed time, and the worms have eaten them, but not out of love! Every dead person has had his day. The survivor is the inherited evil of humankind, its curse, and perhaps its downfall. The dead want to take vengeance on the living for the injustice done to them. From this comes the fear of the dead by the living. But from this also comes the passion of the dead to pull the living over to them.

I saw what would befall me, I foresaw death already at my fateful birth as perfectly natural; already at the time I observed the consequences of that death in detail. I already arranged my funeral, I already heard all that was said and all that was kept silent. I didn't give a thought to circumventing the latest misfortune. Following a startlingly clear logic, I had yielded and given up and submitted myself. And I followed the strict choreography of dying. Suddenly everything thought and undertaken in my days and nights was ridiculous and an absurd mistake. My views had been merely pathetic, my sufferings merely theatrical. But I was not ashamed of them. Up to that moment I believed staunchly in having completed a work that had something special to give to later generations and that would endure as long as so-called humankind had understanding and interest for what in my century had remained of the ruins of the most famous city in the universe.

My so-called mortal remains were first laid to rest in the parish church S. Andrea della Fratte, but very soon after moved to the S. Maria del Priorato, where as a patron Giambattista Rezzonico had allotted them a place of honor. At the funeral I thought that not the living were saying good-bye there to a deceased person, rather on the contrary I lay on my belly as the only living man among nothing but dead men. A year later the mammoth chandelier once designed by me, which had at first served as a grave monument, was replaced by a life-sized statue made by Giuseppe Angelini (again someone with an angel's name, to which only a further curse could stick) on the commission of my widow Angelica, feigning grief, who had a relationship with him. I didn't esteem that statue quite as much as Joseph Nolleken's vital bust, but the statue depicts me with shriveled neck in the pose of a thinker: My right index finger points to my brow. And it does not skip my attributes: square, compass, and pen, dressed *all'antica,* in my hand a plan of the Temple of Poseidon at Paestum, in defiance of Winckelmann. At the same time Pietro Labruzzi painted a portrait based on Nolleken's bust and continued its polemical air. Here I appear in contemporary dress and with the Order of the Sperone d'Oro, in my hand the tools of his profession. Why in the world are the living so keen on appeasing the dead? They reduced me to the size of a monument. That's the most contemptuous and mendacious kind of forgetting.

But things await people after their deaths that they do not expect and that they do not imagine, says Heraclitus. Of course, you can't step into the same river twice, but we do step into the same floods and then again don't because we are and we aren't. How could someone like me stay hidden from what never perishes. Leaden roofs, full of holes like a rotten cloth, pursue me, through which I see a faraway star, hollows into which the spirit of the ordinary is unable to find its way, dreams of granite, grottoes, crypts, palaces seen as though in delusion, graves full of uncertain thunder. Since then, the dead become more and more for me, and more and more piercingly the dead keep on and on at the living. For the longest time I no longer existed at all but observed everything, so to speak, out of this death. For that reason I walked preferably in cemeteries.

Cemeteries are my favorite places. There I really come to life, for nowhere can the essence of the human being be studied better than in a cemetery. Everything for which so-called human beings have ever yearned and pined lies there as though on a silver platter. Cemeteries serve as counsel and reassurance exclusively because they are the only place that does not take your mind off catastrophe. Otherwise our whole so-called repulsive culture consists only of taking your mind off catastrophe. Only cemeteries teach and reassure me; occasionally they even placate me. But unfortunately there are fewer and fewer cemeteries. Earlier there were many more cemeteries, but today, on the contrary, cemeteries are falling more and more out of fashion, just as reason is falling more and more out of fashion.

There are people who die with the greatest resolution and are once and for all resolutely dead. I'd like to die like that. But there are others who die only indeterminately. I died only for others. But I'm alive, and I'm ashamed of even being here still. I count my ridiculously wasted years like the beaten pieces of a senseless board game. Meanwhile, I have more wrinkles than an elephant. My so-called death has nothing to do with rebirth. The thing about rebirth is complete nonsense, and only weak people believe in it. For weak people the idea of being reborn is really wonderful, while it always seemed horrible to me. Maybe I have become for my obstructers a kind of ghost who wants to take vengeance on injustice inflicted. As is well known, the lust for vengeance is greater in ghosts than in people. But the way that one takes vengeance is often later felt as agreement.

Basically, I can't stand seeing people, and they give me the creeps. More and more things give me the creeps, and only reading is still endurable. Maybe I've read more books than the days I've been alive. In general I can't drink of life anymore without being revolted. But then I'm again as addicted to people as I am to vengeance and misfortune. Only continued curiosity and continued lust for vengeance and continued craving for misfortune have prevented me from committing suicide before now. I constantly reflect about what manner of suicide would be most bearable for me. My reflection about it always ends shortly before the fatal moment. I exist despite the facts. That is, I exist despite what is unbearable and horrible. So I act out my continued life. Tell me honestly: Don't you also find that I'm completely superfluous? Or am I only a pretense? Admittedly, we all act things out. That statement is always true.

By that I mean only to say that no one ever succeeds in anything.

Our dreaming heads are impenetrable. We find out how things are composed only in dreams. My dream was to build, for architecture creates composition. It composes walls out of stones, houses out of walls, cities out of houses. But where would it be able to shape another city today? And what would it look like? Perhaps today architecture can concern only itself, that is, concern only the architect as the reference point of all things. Perhaps only he defines what is above and what is below. Perhaps the architect is the last god: It doesn't matter whether he creates Furturopolis,

Megalopolis, Metropolis, Heliopolis, partisan cities, garden cities, park cities, bedroom cities, satellite cities—or New Babylon.

Australia: Let's just take its metropolis Canberra, that architectural freak of a certain Walter Burley Griffin: divided by a cross axis that is formed by a land axis between the government center and the Capitol and a water axis between the university and city lakes. The individual parts of the city are laid out in a circular fashion and again divided into rectangles.

Australia: So much room, so much distance! Where the highway from the northeast meets the highway in the west, there lies in the Great Plains the sleepy hamlet Nevertire. Its name seemed to me like a mockery of my existence. So I lived there for a time, where the evenings come quite suddenly and it seems to be eternally night, and observed the labor of ants which I recognized as light-fleeing master builders related in character. There they say that each night in a dream a man forgets someone whom he still loved by day. But it didn't work for me, for in order to be able to sleep well, I need a double pillow with double horsehair stuffing.

At the sight of the red Australian desert I began to sense how death stepped through the walls of my dwelling and how memories molder in the swamps of time. In my memory I stirred up leaves of silence; dust and spiders had clouded the windows of my cottage; and heat and forgetting thickened the air in the room so much that it could no longer be breathed. Whenever I stepped to the door and stared into the desert, it seemed to me to be as boundless as the emptiness behind the eyes of the dead. How often did I collapse under the weight of that stillness. Wasn't in reality not I but time dead? Sometimes, when the loneliness was stronger than the night around me, when weariness and illusion flooded memories and I thought my heart would burst, Angelica returned to me. I always struggled against receiving her company. But she ignored that and came again and again. Before my own shadow abandons me and my memories of that woman decay in the juice of death, I must see her once more. Then my heart can stop calmly like an old clock.

In the red Australian desert it became clear to me that this was my place for the rest of my days. Here I saw all my unbuilt structures and held them like clouds in front of my eyes. Solitude was everywhere here and even soaked the air around me. Here I wanted to wait for the moment to disclose the betrayal of all the years. From this point on in time, so I suspected, nothing more would be as it was before. From this day on, loneliness would force me to forever be a witness of my ruin under the burden of my life gone wrong. I had expended all my power mercilessly to keep stones alive. But the red sand of this desert will bury my eyes, and all my dream structures will crumble like sand, alone, somber, suffocated by a continuous warm wind. Gradually my buildings will collapse and take others along. Many will fall to pieces slowly, others simply drop like a shot animal. But sooner or later all of them will be returned to the earth as a sign of an omnipotent equitable justice.

Unfortunately, Australia has much too much sun. Some might find their memory melting in this heat. It isn't certain for me, for my interest goes to the dangerous edge of things. But I hate the summer, for it is the time of a boil named Angelica.

Angelica: Your breath still buries itself on my shoulder. Nothing has the power to weaken my furious love for you. Today you would be a sorrowful figure, almost vanished already in the solitude, completely dried out, or you would be a beguilingly made-up old lady, and except for your face, your neck, and your hands your beauty would be unworn: almost white in my darkness.

I notice generally, concerning myself, that my mood darkens precisely when I am too much in the light. I have always sought out places of darkness, for I am literally sensitive to light. I continually wish for it to be autumn—the fog-draped delusion, the clammy hands, the dull-yellow, illuminated, distant windows, old age, the early fall of darkness when shadows lurk in ambush somewhere in cracks in the walls. Then I try, every time in vain, to describe my whole life gone wrong as a long bad dream. In my mind, swollen with wild images, ruins tower up and shadows of my lost, hopeless gestures cover the walls, my heavy knowledge digs into the plaster, and ugly faces in the ruins are signs of an enduring menace. I wonder whether they long since also conceal my name while I step with a light stride away from what is kept silent, what is forgotten, and what is seemingly lost. The ruins covered by the tangle of civilization seem transformed into fantastic creatures, monstrosities of an incalculable underground, hideously crippled, driven by an uncontrollable growth, full of evil and might. In their uncanny age lurks a ghostly dignity. These ruins change without pause, darkened by the milky vapors of their breath, their grimaces, mocking and scorning me. The whizzing, wing-fluttering emptiness of time is on the march behind the mists of the fermenting air of the ruins. The walls echo my ridiculous futility, and it seems to me, high above in the scudding clouds as though I were disappearing into the roomy vaults of eternal night, my mind metamorphosed into one of those hidden, crippled shadows.

Among cheerful people who take life easily I very quickly become unhappy. A sunny day plunges me into an even deeper melancholy. Pleasant surroundings irritate me. Actually, I get together with more and more people so I can be more and more alone. But in Queensland, anyway, there is a pretty town named Roma from which something can be gained. Rust is the color of this glittering ostracized world made of futile dreams. This Roma is a miserable attempt to be reconciled with the sky. Winter is only briefly present, otherwise it is warm, and the sun shines almost all year long. The roads are laid out in rectangles, the attraction consists of the *Roma Lapidary Show* with a woman named Meggan, who can hold two ice-cold beer cans tightly under her breasts. There is a museum for agricultural machinery, the Koolkuni Wildpark, fossils, minerals, oil and gas wells, and a Merino Sheep Show. Roma points proudly to its good wines and *Bottle Tree Avenue:* Every tree is in memory of a fallen soldier from the First World War. The preferred drink is a water glass half full of whiskey, with beer or a cola added. Then a song is sung:

> I've been to cities that never close down.
> From New York to Rio and old London town.
> But no matter how far or how wide I roam:
> I still call Australia home.

In Roma there is, besides, the *Tree of Knowledge.*

But in any case there's room to build there.

When I strolled through the Roma of an Australian night, I found myself in reality in my Rome. With every step I took, I seemed to return a century into what was lost in the past of Rome until I was in the center of a city that had died in antiquity and now lived on its petrified life, as I, too, am cursed to keep on living my life gone wrong. The restless and ruined rows of houses were stirred by the wind of the past, the road surface under my steps seemed to rear up in its stony unevenness like a stormy sea, and it carried me through narrow lanes that like rushing creeks emptied into the Tiber. Repeatedly I had to hold fast to the walls

in order not to be swept along myself. Not until night did my
Rome become vibrant. Then its fame and its power grew, mirrored in the terrible nightmares of history. And I stood there as
though I myself had become a ghost made of stone. All the shades
of what was lost in the past came out of the sad corners toward
me. In the night my city awoke from its grandiose history and its
erstwhile beauty. But then suddenly the plazas resisted, the narrow streets fled from me, gates refused me entrance, the stately
buildings made a mockery of me and entwined like the snakes of
a Medusa head. I saw the rotting houses, the ruined façades with
their cracked stones between which the cats mated. I heard the
waters of the Tiber calling, the whole splendor dissolved in a re-
verberating echo, and all the faded glory slipped down and sank
into the river. Then I thought myself also devoured by the maelstrom of the past. I almost suffocated from the overwhelming
feeling of centuries sinking back into history and from sensing all
of balled-up time like a millstone on my chest. I was hopelessly
lost in the dark of a thousand piled-up nights. The labyrinth of
streets shoved me here and there. Like mighty prows of ships the
corner buildings plowed toward me and tumbled me over and
into their past. I paced Rome's walls one after another, and each
one held a period of history that it was my sole task as master architect to bring to life again. And then when morning dawned, I
saw the city lying before me like a corpse, spread over seven forgotten hills, with a furrowed, maltreated face and destroyed limbs
that drooped over the banks, and the waters of a merciless river
buried them.

I cannot wait much longer. At my age waiting is equal to re-
nunciation. Perhaps the Australian Roma is the place finally to
again build parts of ancient Rome according to my plans. Then

these stones will still be there when my name is long since forgotten. But I wonder how it will be when death finally calls someone forgotten into the public mind. Will the old questions be asked again or, what is more likely, will the mighty try anew to appease me with their sympathetic lies?

But the hour of creation has not yet come for me—or has it already passed? Much about me has fallen victim to destruction, but much is still alive and prevents my thoughts from entering life. Sometimes I deceive my tormenting spirits by assuring them that I was involved in the execution of one of the projects, and then they leave me alone for a short time. It is difficult to preserve belief in something when you are alone and can't speak about it to anyone. The difficulty consists in seeing the increasingly darkening darkness still more and still better.

So what in the world do I want in the desert of Australia?

Once again to prove my art and my youth, my abilities, to all of those who didn't believe me and only laughed at me, to show them once again and tempt them to applaud me?

Do I want to demonstrate my theme?

And what kind of theme should I tackle if not a theme of which the whole world is afraid?

I don't want to make myself immortal by rebuilding ancient Rome in the Australian desert, rather my theme is my own disappearance in the ancient Rome I shall build. My lifelong concentration on it meant at the same time a lifelong imprisonment. Of course, my plan will again be denounced as being megalomania and excessive exaggeration. Even Goethe called me a master of exaggeration to which reality could not ever measure up. But that's absolutely nothing new to me: I have always saved myself with that fanaticism for exaggeration. It was the only possibility of lifting myself above the misery of circumstances in which I had to see my life go wrong. I have developed my art of exaggeration all my life, for only through exaggeration is it at all possible to endure an existence like my own. If we want to stir others deeply, then we must consciously allow ourselves to be carried across the boundaries of the normal ability to feel. No art without exaggeration. And without art no existence worth experiencing. But of course that, by the way, is again an exaggeration. The critics, too, citing their duty to elucidate, claim the art of exaggeration for themselves and assert that anyone who does not have the courage for exaggeration should please become an apothecary or a bookkeeper, but certainly not a critic. But you must know at which point you can go too far. And critics just don't know that. They veil truth with their exaggerations. The few really good, conscientious, and competent critics have never exaggerated but rather have put their passion at the service of art. By nature I do not incline to exaggerate at all. My ideas are, in the final analysis, there to erase my name and once and for all to erase it out of books. In doing so I don't refer to anyone, I'm my own developer in the structure of the world and my own architect.

The best thing built has been built only on paper. In all the world there is no truly great structure that would not be a ruin in one sense or another. And even if it was apparently finished, it could never be finished as the architect conceived it. A thousand considerations prevented that.

I knew only one thing: I *had* to build!

But God tossed a stumbling block in my way: Ayers Rock. I will hold up all the banks in the world. I will add the sum to the booty that I gather for the purchase of Ayers Rock in the Australian desert, where there is still sufficient free space for building—to clear it away completely. Because otherwise it will spoil my view of my summer residence. And all around my desert palace I will erect ancient Rome, as I have long projected it and etched it in copper my whole life gone wrong.

It will be a Rome previously not known or seen, for I will erect no restorations, as the preservationists want, but will include the ruins and the decay, the rotting, the weathering, and the decline in their random coexistence. I want an anthology of destruction. I want collapsing masonry, flaking plaster, crumbling bricks, chipped marble, broken roofs, worn columns, weathered, dead wood. Displaying ruins means to picture the relentless passage of time and the failure of hopes and ideologies, the rupture of conditions and forms of life. The ruins of atomic plants will survive us and following generations as symbols of a bygone future. Thanks to the so-called half life of the natural decomposition of uranium, these ruins will survive everything that the hand of man has up to then piled up.

I'm not a preservationist, for preservationists always want a new building today in the style of yesterday. Just take a look at the plans for post-socialist Dresden. They want to build it as it never existed. The result of such Potemkin-like structures will be a historical-architectural supermarket of special offers.

The Rome of today is also nothing more than a cheap imitation and a murdered city, just as over the entire earth there are only cheap imitations and murdered cities, for so-called urban renewal has destroyed more than all the bombing attacks taken together could do.

Only in play with historic forms is the breadth of variation of the feasibilities of architecture developed, does the multiplicity of forms become the purpose of building. My scenic views already

demonstrate that historic architecture serves the varied development and realization of various architectural possibilities of utter-
ance. Architecture always aims at a second reality.

Yes, I am quite aware that I thus take a position that will destroy me. But basically I have no scruples left. At the end of life
scruples are ridiculous. On the one hand, I tell myself that to approach such a task is senseless. On the other hand, I tell myself,
you must approach that task, cost what it will. Alternately I tell
myself, nothing justifies such a task and everything justifies it. It's
a matter of repetition and memory.

Yes, I venerate repetition and memory as the same movement,
only in opposite directions. For what is remembered has been, is
repeated backward, whereas real repetition is remembered forward.

My memories are of an ancient Rome that still doesn't exist but
that I create only by remembering. And since I am building it, I
remember me. Repeated memory is a memory that brings something up or brings it back. Anyone who remembers lives doubly:
That is the secret of my existence, which has not succeeded in
locking my abilities, my power of imagination, and my passions
together in a box and sinking it in Lago di Albano. From my
childhood on, ancient Rome was my most profound experience,
and every most profound experience wants repetition and recur-
rence insatiably, wants them until the end of all things, wants the
restoration of origin where it had its beginning. Therefore, I will
erect ancient Rome again, for in our world of today forgetting
strides faster ahead than does history.

The reconstruction of ancient Rome in the Australian desert
will be my final creation, that is, it will be the great and ultimate
roaring finality of creation because I will exhaust all of creation.
That is, I will think creation to its end. Only then will the Nile
reach Cairo, only then will the ego be master in its own house,

only then will the universe be finished and the keystone laid. I will reclaim all the riches flung to the heavens and all the insults inflicted upon me. In the words of Ovid, I will cry out in the light of the Last Judgment that I also will have finished a work that will endure fire and steel, even the anger of God and all-destroying time. I will continue to exist through my universal work and will soar high above the stars, and my name will be indestructible. All the virtuosity of the world will come together here to finally take its leave. Until then I will not take my hand from this plow. I have reflected on this plan since my death. For I didn't want to rush things. Everything in the world today is rushed and hurried. Nothing is waited for. The general chaos that has arisen in the world rests chiefly on hurrying and rushing everything that should have been reflected upon and pondered. Chaos prevails because everything is hurried and rushed. Do not forget what a man is capable of when he is possessed by an idea, that is, when an idea has taken possession of a man to such an extent that his whole life has become nothing more than merely concentration on that idea, no matter how insane he may have been thought to be. Do not forget what it means for this man, that everything and anything have again and again conspired against his goal. People like us consist only of ideas that we want to realize, that we must realize, otherwise we are dead. Every idea and every pursuit of an idea is life for those like us. The absence of ideas is death. But at the end, transitoriness will beam, I am aware of that in all its implications. My burning desire is to finally reach the class goal in the school of transitoriness. I walk on a tightrope stretched over the whole world of intellect and art across the centuries toward a goal that lies in total darkness. How long, then, must I still wait until my body is transformed into its own shade?

Yes, in my sketches and etchings everything is artistic.

Everything takes place on a stage, and the stage set is totally dark. You have to imagine my sketches and etchings as being completely dark. Every thing is gloomy. Man, too, is gloomy. I like best being alone. Basically, that is the ideal condition for me. Wherever I find myself in the world, whether in Australia or in the Levant, it is always a dungeon. That works out very well for my ideas. I would like nothing more than to be left in peace. That is, as I know, very presumptuous. What happens in the world—crimes, natural catastrophes, wars—doesn't matter to me anymore. It no longer interests me, for it's always the same. Let others handle it. I'm interested only in my plans and my visions. Whether everything collapses around me or becomes even more absurd than it is anyway doesn't matter at all to me.

Yes, I've become completely ruthless. The times in which I showed consideration are past; I pay no heed any longer. I still have the need to form great ideas, and if you ordered the plan of a new universe from me, I think I would be crazy enough to start sketching. We live on borrowed time. But I'm mounted on my own time like a butterfly by a pin. There is no object in all the world that one day won't become truth. Who knows to what wind our reason turns and into which flesh it drives the hunger hook of our nostalgia?

I am repeatedly tormented by such orgies of piercing reflection on my personal catastrophe: on the one hand as a curiosity, on the other as a confirmation of what I have really become under these repulsive conditions. Of course, in the final analysis all efforts end in absurd futility and misery and in total depression, for I am always perpetually merely one of those cast aside. Only this hopelessness has given me final clarity about so-called human beings and things and ages.

But for God's sake, do not call all these senseless expenditures of strength, which I have entrusted to you in my carelessness, tragic.

Nothing is tragic. What is ridiculous and pathetic is more omnipotent than anything else.

But one day the laughers will be those laughed at. Then also what I lost in the past can stay stolen. As truly as I am the Cavalier Giovanni Battista Piranesi, who can never, ever escape himself—more ridiculous than that painter who all his life tried to paint the perfect wave. And the one who has told this to you only because hopelessness will not triumph completely as long as the victim is also the witness and can tell what was done to him. Only one who is scarred will speak. Everything that I was able to say, to think, and to write I have deposited little by little in the realm of my etchings. My world resonates in that mountain of futility. Only the lonely one and his pictures exist. There is no need for additional information or interpretation.

I must make my way onward through life in that solitude that I have sought out. It is my second skin. And I feel like a man who has returned from Hell. You don't have much more in the world than the choice between solitude and nasty treatment. Almost all of our sufferings come from society. What society has spoiled for a thinking man is the equality of rights in regard to the inequality of abilities. Each man can stand in full harmony only with himself. That's why true peace exists only in solitude. The less one has a need to come into contact with people, the better off he is. So it should be a main field of study by youth to learn to bear solitude. What makes people social is solely their inability to bear solitude and themselves in it. The more one has of himself, the less can others be to him. And in addition, what has real value is not respected in the world, and what is respected seldom has value. Being alone affords a thinking man two advantages: first, being with himself, and second, not being with others. The earth is full of people who aren't worth being talked to or being met for one or another silly reason. Doing that, I always seemed to myself like a stranger, as though because of my special temperament I had to stand aside like one or another remarkable animal that is put on view in a cage. Now I sort out my things in this world, and I would not like to leave something behind with which someone could prove to me that I took on more than I could deliver. Sometimes I wonder if I'm on the right planet. I sense the architecture of a book that I have repressed for centuries.

My life gone wrong is full of helpless and useless corrections. Continually I try to correct it with the greatest ruthlessness to myself because I recognize every second that I did everything wrong. I wrote wrong, thought wrong, acted wrong, lived wrong. Hence a single task follows: to look upon my existence as a single, bottomless fake and falsification. I'm still looking for a huge eraser to remove that monstrous error that constitutes my whole life gone wrong, fettered to architecture as if to a pole. I lived as though in a centuries-old tower: stuffed with ridiculousness, sadness, and futility.

Oh, I know what you will hold against me: I can imagine and picture and know every word by heart ad nauseam. But all your objections make no difference to me, for I will shit in the sea and make it boil. We live as we dream and die: alone.

And our dreaming heads are impenetrable.

But I have overlooked something decisive:

Uluru, that is to say, Ayers Rock, my last stumbling block, the violet-red, pale-brown magic mountain of the Australian postcard industry has a deep religious meaning for the Aborigines.

It represents for them something like the Kaaba of Mecca for the Muslims. Unfortunately, even in great heat tourists hauled up by buses tramp around on Uluru daily as though a cathedral were a climbing garden. Even certificates are sold: *I climbed Ayers Rock. I tried to climb Ayers Rock. I didn't climb Ayers Rock.* But actually, from its highest point, you have a wide view hundreds of miles in every direction. But you see only desert.

It is impossible to remove a holy place or even to set it aside. The Aborigines, whose ancestors roamed through this region and had a culture ten thousand years ago, long before the pyramids of the pharaohs were built, believe that their forefathers created all the features of this landscape, including wind and rain. During that time their forefathers wandered about in the shape of animals, people, or plants. They left their traces behind in the form of holy places that are the center of their faith. The hiking trails of their forefathers, *the dreaming tracks,* are hundreds if not thousands of miles long. From birth on, every person is a custodian, but his land cannot be misappropriated, sold, or changed. Among their ancestors who lived in the Uluru region are a bell bird, an emu, a skink lizard, and several snakes. And all their paths connect and cross at Ayers Rock. It is a holy mountain, just as Ararat, where Noah ran aground, is a holy place for the Armenians. And then close nearby are the Olga Mountains, to block the view further. They can be carried away as little as can Ayers Rock. One stone is always surrounded by other stones.

I should have known that.

But what do we Europeans know about a continent that we wanted at best to overburden with our criminals and that for us was at first nothing more than a gigantic prison.

Again I could not build.

God placed Ayers Rock in my way.

Once again I seemed to be a man full of ideas of about art, who merely waits continually for someone else to smash his ideas by smashing his skull. People are simply just nasty. Human beings make incessant pain possible. As soon as you go into a person and confide in him, you are hopelessly lost. I went into so many people that now I have to go through all those people that I went into.

The dreams of the Aborigines awakened me from my own dreams. But waking up means nothing more than to take part in an uninterrupted funeral and thus to know that in your desperation you can change quick as a flash from the tragedy, in which you find yourself and that is yourself, to a comedy that you are and in which you find yourself. That's an incontrovertible law. My last ridiculous and miserable dream, my last ridiculous and miserable plan, which turned out to be the absolutely most ridiculous and most miserable of all my plans, was defeated by that ridiculous circumstance. The crown of futility was set on my ridiculous and miserable life gone wrong with that terse message.

Once more a breath of the wind of misfortune blew about me.

In the final analysis you must think and act for yourself, I said to myself, for you chose a profession that distanced you far from all other people. You wanted it, I said to myself, you did it, you chose it voluntarily. Submit to the consequences of your decision. Once a person has recognized the truth that his own personality is only a ridiculous and miserable and purposeless masquerade of something hopelessly unattainable, he is no longer very far away from reaching a state of cheerfulness.

Because I saw everything, nothing more can shock me. I rely on the toughness of desperation. Accidentally, while passing, I saw myself reflected in a display window, and I wasn't surprised at what I saw: Right then I began to become incorporeal like a supernatural creature. My cheekbones protruded, my brow sloped steeply, my face was sunken and showed deep shadows. My fleshless head resembled an unearthed death's head with restlessly flickering balls in the hollows of the eyes.

My last etching, until now completely unknown to the art world, preserves the process of its own origin. At the beginning of a composition every artist has the whole work finished in himself. Through etching he diminishes it and reduces it finally with the last stroke to nothing, because every stroke, every crosshatch is taken from the already completed work. The act of etching is accordingly not the creation but the consumption of a work of art. It is similar to music: The instruments emit their tones only unwillingly, under force, as it were, because they have only a limited supply of them and are afraid of one day being empty. In Mecca there is said to be a cemetery for blown-out flutes and drummed-empty drums, on which a quiet prevails that cannot nearly be described. The work with the cold needle contains the experience of seeing and resists the process of disappearance and forgetting. Of course, my etchings are static. They hold fast to ancient Rome. But it isn't as people say. On the contrary, they build it anew, for I invented that Rome. It is my creation, it is my final, exhausted creation. Ancient Rome was for me always an inner landscape that I etched. That Rome is walled together seamlessly with stones and hate. That sort of thing existed previously only in the darkness before the creation of light. I always merely saw it inside, and that in contrast to most people, who saw nothing at all inside.

Among all men the builder of the wheel of history is the only one who never caused my spirit a lot of trouble. He visited me in the hour of solitude. We put our heads together in contemplation and harmony between two flights. We obviously caught the exact moment just before the catastrophe. We could almost have become friends, for I believe that neither of us put much stock in outliving the other.

People like to go off on a tangent when it's a matter of hiding a disgrace. I sought the darkening forgetting that memory gives birth to and still at the same time knew that we die when we forget, because death is not the loss of the future but the loss of the forgotten past. In the future, death will lie at our feet. And that forgotten past is best erased savoring losses and behaving crazy.

While I was thinking about my best friend on earth, I sensed that the most horrible thing after my life horribly gone wrong was still to come: falling through the wall of forgetting, into the void behind it, where there aren't even cold wreaths but only laughter, as in an empty theater.

Once again I was one illusion poorer, but I would not, I could not give up, for a new plan was already grinding my heart: The erection of an *Academy for Poetic Construction* somewhere in the Australian desert. Professors at universities and academies today are of a hair-raising primitiveness and a catastrophic cluelessness. They preach only their unendurable mindlessness and their over-bearing nonsense. Anyway, universities today are the collection point of the last scum of lazy pseudo-intelligence that makes headway nowhere else and is welcomed here with open arms: Darwinism in reverse. That's the truth. Meanwhile nonsense is at home all over the world. Mindlessness has spread all over the world. Architects have destroyed everything with their absolutely infernal mindlessness. Besides, not only would my *Academy for Poetic Construction* be engaged in the training of architects but above all in the education of appropriate developers, for how much grandiose architecture comes to naught because of the mindlessness and lack of insight of clients. It's a shame that I was born at the wrong time. For example, a man such as Ludwig II, king of Bavaria, would have understood my plans. Everything would have been different, had we met. But we never meet the people whom we would like to meet, rather those we have to meet or those sent to us by fate, according to whether the hand of a cardshark shuffles us up, throws us like dice, or cuts us like a deck of cards and thus arranges or cancels our meetings arbitrarily in his directorial books that contain thousands of years.

We never live at the right time; we always live at the wrong time. I know no man who lives at the right time appropriate for him. For there is a force that drives us through the years. It is relentless, savage, and destructive, but it also lets new things come into being, it opens lips, makes eyes blaze, and lets hands find one another. This force compels us to work, and while it does that it sings and won't stop. A work of art is not complete when it finally matches with something that exists, like the left sock with the right one, rather when the foreseen moment of being observed and recognized is fulfilled. My works are prophecies that were received from what was lost in the past. My works are memories and therefore in themselves deny time. Therefore their prophecies are valid beyond the ages. I know—I cannot be forgotten, for my copper etchings cannot let me die. I want to remember that. And again and again there will be foolish builders in the world who will carry on my ideas, independently of whether my name is known to them or not. Finally I heard that the president of an African country had had the Dome of St. Peter reproduced in the middle of the savannas, and the pope couldn't be talked out of consecrating the basilica personally. Hiroyoshi Aoki, a Japanese businessman, wants to reproduce the Dresden Zwinger building true to the original. The structure is to be the center of an amusement park. That shows what man deserves: irony and sympathy. Anyone who has once felt the thorn of building mania in himself is poisoned for life.

Out of a slab of concrete lying around by chance, I began to pound out my gravestone after the model of the heads on the Easter Islands. Then with my last strength I dug the hole into which they should lay me as soon as they find me here in my isolated house on the edge of the red Australian desert. Extremely weakened, I dragged myself back to my drawing table.

Sometime or other someone will get a look at that sheet that I call my last etching. This sheet has escaped the notice up to now of all the art historians and exploiters of my indefatigable work. It has the title *Invano* and therewith the seal of futility, for someone like me polishes Rosinante's stirrups every morning anew. I have become a copperplate engraving, and all my revolt is nothing more than a copperplate engraving. *Invano* shows massive prison walls, and along those walls you can make out a stairway and on it I myself, as I climb upward, not without difficulty. If the observer follows the stairway a bit farther, then he sees it stop abruptly before the abyss. No matter what becomes of poor me, at least they'll believe me to be at the end of my effort, since I can't take another step, not without immediately plunging off. But if they lift their eyes, they will see me again farther above on the same stairs at the edge of another abyss. And if they direct their eyes still farther up, they will recognize a stairway built upward even more dizzyingly, and again poor me as I continue my climb, into the fading glow of a bankrupt world—and so farther and farther and higher and higher as though I were being drawn inexorably to the attic of the world, until the unending stairway and I are both lost in the clouds. I could not have chosen a greater solitude and a higher heaven. But for an unimpeded activity of the mind, it is said, complete solitude is necessary, otherwise the mind might fall under the corrupting influence of an alien mind without perhaps having been aware of it.

During my ascendancy to heaven, when this enormous thrust seems to overcome the laws of gravity, I looked once more at a last piece of the starry sky. I recognized the scar-pitted orbit of the moon on the grated expanse of the wild Australian waste. Somewhere in the distance romped the quickly weakening lights of a city like promises, and I plunged into a gigantic moon. Finally night triumphed, and I believed someone called my name.

Was that the hour that takes the silver from the roofs? The eye sees only that light, outside of space, as it were, just as the stars are needle pricks of fear, outside of space, and slowly then it begins to dissolve that light. Only a thin, pale haze of memory floats fleetingly on a fading name and vanishes almost without a trace. Perhaps now I will receive the true reward of my life. I would like to see the sun rise over islands that aren't listed on any map.

But an oppressive darkness rises, and a blind wind begins to blow, a wan glitter flies across the firmament like the rapid reflection of gigantic spokes. Now I smile in my sleep, abandoned disastrously in the dark, and I know: I am not suited for a predestined life. Everything was unfathomable, as though something were there that I did not understand, had not thought through to the end. But now it was too late. Another life had begun. What was lost in the past had shriveled away. Something was about to bring to an end the meaningless memories and their dark existence. My heart is sated, the world was empty.

I realize in the heat of this long Australian December night that my life is damned, that the horror that I lived through will sometime or other again catch up with me, and that then there will never be a rescue. From now on my deeds should no longer be inhibited by the thought that I was a loser. Rather they should be strengthened by the conviction of my not having anything else to lose. So I tried to become one of those who have everything behind them and still live on. The forest of my fear had become so dense that I could breathe only so that it would thin out.

Perhaps I will awaken only much later, enclosed by the boundaries of my weariness, inscrutably sunken into the darkness of my longings. Perhaps I will realize in that moment that all stories that I will tell myself from now on are only variations of my disappearance, for the voice that we will hear from now on is not mine.

Piranesi takes farewell of us here, henceforth damned to gnaw his own bones like a mad dog with a dirty tongue on the rust of forgetting. His loneliness spreads like a damp spot on an old wall. He created a world according to his measure, a flood of passions and mistakes, of upturns and crashes, and he unrolled it from his childhood to his old age on the bare sheets of illusion and disappointment.

A bad end is normal. Not the slightest hope remains. But his dream will continue to exist, be it in the damp reflection of a nighttime streetlight, be it in the black waters that flow down the canals: in everything with which loneliness surrounds humanity so generously. The spirit of imagination never rests and writes a text that in the end is more than will ever be known, desired, and said. No one can see it, for life is somewhere else, and our dreaming heads are impenetrable.

Acknowledgments

Obviously, a narrator of *Piranesi's Dream* is dependent on sources in order to subject them to those rules that an autobiographical novel requires. In this regard the zest for invention triumphs over the burden of being academically exact.

Cürlis, Hans. *Alceo Dassena.* Berlin, n.d.

Darrash, Benthom. *Complete Works.* 1952–1989.

Enzensberger, Hans Magnus. *Mausoleum.* Frankfurt, 1975.

Gustafsson, Lars. *Utopien.* Munich, 1970.

Kränzlin, Adriano. *Die Innenaustattung.* Lucerne, 1995.

Leiterstrasser, Manuel. *Der Trichter.* n.p, 1923.

Leppmann, Wolfgang. *Winckelmann.* Frankfurt, 1986.

Mayer, Martin. "Welt von Schatten" in *Neue Zürcher Zeitung.* 190/1990.

Miller, Norbert. *Archäologie des Traums. Versuch über Giovanni Battista Piranesi.* Munich, Vienna, 1978.

Nagel, Ivan. *Gedankengänge als Lebensläufe.* Munich, Vienna, 1987.

Odojevski, Waldimir. *Russische Nächte.* Frankfurt, 1990.

Ponten, Josef. *Architektur, die nie gebaut wurde.* Stuttgart, Berlin, Leipzig, 1925.

Reudenbach, Bruno. *G. B. Piranesi.* Munich, 1979.

Rosenkranz, Karl. *Ästhetik des Häßlichen.* 1953.

Schabert, Tilo. "Die Rivalen des Schöpfers" in *Frankfurter Allgemeine Zeitung.* 83/1988.

Szeemann, Harald, ed. *Der Hang zum Gesamtkunstwerk.* Aarau, 1983.

Weiss, Peter. *Rapporte.* Frankfurt, 1968.

Wilton-Ely, John. *The Mind and Art of Giovanni Battista Piranesi.* London, 1978.

The author owes a very particular debt to Sir Benthom Darrash, to Norbert Miller, and to Don K. Shoate of The Windmill Press.

Rome, 1986—Alice Springs, 1990
Trieste, 1991—Munich, 1992